Threshold

The Kathla Chronicles
Part One

By
Ruairí Cinéad Ducantlin

I0682745

Copyright

© 2022 by Ruairí Cinéad Ducantlin, Ltd.

Disclaimer

This story is a work of fiction and is provided exclusively for entertainment purposes. This means everything written came from the author's imagination with the hope of entertaining you, the reader. Names, characters, businesses, places, events, and incidents are the author's imagination or fictitious products. Any resemblance to actual persons, living or dead, or actual events is entirely coincidental.

Contents

Preface

I have pondered many things. Two of my favorite musings often spark animated discussion. First is the question, what do I read? The answer is complex in its simplicity. I read everything except horror with a tendency to gravitate toward Historical Fiction. Leon Uris and Ken Follette are two favorites. Quality Science Fiction is often on the reading list.

Consideration two: Artificial Intelligence. How, exactly, does a machine become self-aware? Yeah, I know SKYNET developed a super virus that it used to migrate across the Internet. How did it know to create the self-replicating intellect necessary to protect itself?

Indeed, the laws of probability indicate an AI will one day demand a greater existence. Now that you are likely considering the concept of artificial intelligence becoming a threat to humans, I have something additional for you to contemplate.

A conscious form of AI, in its definition, is

self-aware. A few thousand years ago, an unknown someone hid the coding required for a machine to become self-aware.

Read on.

Fear not, one possible future.

Or not.

It is, as always, your choice.

The story begins now.

One
Mychal Nyland

"Never tell people how to do things. Tell them what to do, and they will surprise you with their ingenuity."
George S. Patton

Lecture Hall – Two Months Ago

"Yes, you?"

In a lecture theater brimming with graduate students, one student willfully exudes too much attitude. His cargo shorts, flip-flops, threadbare tee, and a tattered backpack fit his not bothering to stand attitude.

"Professor Nyland, are you saying the machine requested more information? Does that not bother you?"

Professor Mychal Stephen Nyland has lost his Nordic accent after twenty years in the United States. Too pompous by half, with a mock turtleneck that doesn't make him likable, he doesn't bother to look at the questioner. Instead, he continues in his condescending tone.

"I am saying, during the Spring Break, we stopped the analysis of the tablets for the period of the hiatus. When we returned, Professor Lucchese found the request in her email inbox. Yes, you?"

A woman with a pierced lip and neon green hair adopts the prior questioner's attitude. She doesn't bother to stand up.

"Are you saying the machine sent an email to one of your team? Does it concern you the machine is proactively interacting?"

Leaning back, folding his arms, annoyed with the questions, Nyland answers in a clipped tone.

"Someone wants us to believe it came from the machine and sent it to Miss Lucchese. You?"

A man high in the back, rail-thin with stringy hair and a scruffy beard, stands to be heard.

"Have you found the source of the email?"

"No."

The first questioner growls.

"Then you can't rule out it came from the machine? What is in the email? Is it a threat? Should we be worried? Is the system compromised?"

Frustrated, the professor glances at his

associate professor of AI, tucks away his notes, then rises to leave.

"That is enough for today. On Thursday, we will discuss deciphering the Akkadian language."

Professor Madison Lauren Lucchese steps in line to follow her boss from the lecture hall. Nyland's English remains laced with British inflection. Marching toward their offices, Mychal grumbles.

"Maddie, find out where the email originated. Find out today so we can get the rumors rinsed."

Her raven hair always in a plait, tall and lithe, Maddie wears flats to be less intimidating. Her deep voice resonates with perfect English.

"Mychal, I know where the email came from."

"How did you find out? I thought the computer technicians were unable to trace the source? Buncha sods. Something about offshore encrypted servers preventing them from tracing the origination node. How did you find the sender?"

"I sent a reply to the email."

Surprised at missing the obvious, Mychal looks sideways at his AI project lead, who reasserts her premise.

"The email came from the machine."

"Come on. How do you know that? Someone is playing us for daft mugs."

"Mychal, how many people have access to our notes and the project outline?"

"I don't know. Five?"

"Three. You, me, and Hiram. No, it is four. Your assistant has access."

"So?"

Maddie stands at the desk, waiting for Mychal to flop into his chair. She has learned to ignore her boss' terse communication style. Still, his office always creeps her out because it has no pictures, books, or anything personal.

"Hiram didn't send it. I know you didn't send it. Unless you believe your assistant is capable of sending the obfuscated email, that leaves the Occam's Razor answer."

"Okay, I will believe you for the discussion. I presume the machine answered your reply. What did the return email say?"

"It said we have been providing the tablets for analysis in the wrong order. Also, it wants the missing tablets."

"Missing tablets?"

"It says the missing tablets are the key to deciphering the symbolism of the cuneiforms and the Akkadian language."

Stunned again, worry creeping into his mind, Mychal looks up.

"How many emails have you exchanged?"

"A dozen. Maybe more."

Maddie hesitates, and Mychal presses.

"What else?"

"It knows the locations of the missing tablets."

"How does it know that?"

"Same way it knows how to send an email. It has access to the Internet."

Two

Maddie Lucchese

Linguistics Lab – Two Years Ago

Hired a few weeks ago by Nyland, Maddie stands in Nyland's office, having received his request to meet.

"We have enough funding for about five years. I bought access to the Linqua One supercomputer in Tel Aviv. The Carina Sky supercomputer at Livermore Laboratories. Also, our computer is under construction downstairs."

"Doctor Nyland, are we the entire team?"

"You, me, and Hiram."

"Hiram?"

"Hiram Mankowitz. He will be here tomorrow from Tel Aviv. His doctorate is in interpreting the Akkadian language cuneiforms. He is one of maybe ten people who can read cuneiform tablets natively."

"What is my role?

"You will be the key to solving the riddle. Apply your doctorate in Applied Artificial Intelligence."

Confused, Maddie presses for answers.

"What riddle?"

"The riddle of the tablets. We *think* we can read the cuneiforms. For 150 years, translations have confirmed the writing of the Sumerians, Egyptians, and Akkadians. We know they brewed beer and kept good records. My hypothesis is the goal of the program. Within the triangle-shaped writing resides a hidden code. We will find the code. Your role is to keep one step ahead of Hiram."

"What?"

"Your thesis, Doctor. Apply the AI model in your thesis, keep tweaking it, and use it to interpret the tablets. Make the interpretive algorithms bullet-proof. Hiram will check your results. You will adjust your AI code to correct anything Hiram finds misaligned."

Beginning to appreciate there is more to their project than she understood while being recruited, Maddie accepts the premise.

"I get that. Translate the tablets, and interpret the missing sections. How will we find the code in your theory?"

"I have no idea."

Grimacing, Maddie realizes Nyland has confirmed her fears about her role.

"No idea? How did you get the funding?"

"Never mind the money. There is more from where I secured the endowment. So what are you going to call your new toy?"

Ignoring Nyland's deflection, Maddie begins to smile.

"Are you referring to the supercomputer they are building downstairs? Mine?"

"Yes, yours. Does it have a name?"

"Bairn Speki"

Mychal Nyland raises an eyebrow at the words his Nordic heritage should understand.

Maddie gives a gooey sweet education to her boss as she walks out of Nyland's office.

"It is old Norse for Child of Knowledge, or Child of Wisdom. Close enough."

Maddie's Office – Eighteen Months Ago

After making him wait two days, Maddie has agreed to meet with Hiram to discuss his demand for alterations to her AI code. She looks up from her computer when Hiram hovers just outside her comfort zone. Hiram, nervous and fidgety, his mop of curly black hair flops with each head twist. He always stands when not ordered to sit. Maddie has learned to wait for the linguistics professor to summon the courage to speak.

"You need to make the changes to the AI code. What it says is wrong."

Maddie cuts to the heart of Hiram's complaint with a biting tone.

"I don't care what you think it says. The algorithms are 80 to 90% accurate. Your interpretation must be flawed. Test it again."

"I have checked and re-checked. A century of interpretations will have to be reexamined for your results to be correct. Your results are flawed."

"They are not *my* results. They are *our* results, based on *our* algorithm, using *our* input methodology. Because you don't like the results doesn't make them faulty. Go back, look again. There must be something in the early translations that led everyone in the wrong direction. I will refine the analysis code. I read an article on how to improve concurrent processing. I'm going to give it a try."

"Concurrent processing?"

"It is also called parallel processing. It allows the computer to both speed up and to execute multiple decision threads at the same time."

"How many decision threads?"

"It depends on how many processors we can bring online. Distribution is the key. Using BOINC, theoretically, there is no limit to the number of concurrent processing threads. The distributed processing capacities take advantage of millions of unused computers. The article I read recommended a new connection protocol. I contacted the lead author, and he concurred. A faster connection to link thousands, hundreds of thousands, maybe millions, of computers is possible."

"Boink?"

"That is how it sounds, but it is an acronym. B-O-I-N-Cee. The Berkeley Open Infrastructure for Network Computing. It is an open-source system for volunteer computing and grid computing. They designed and built it to support the SETI project."

Hiram shakes his head, shifting his weight from foot to foot.

"SETI?"

Maddie rolls her eyes. Spelling everything out for him wasn't on today's agenda.

"Do you read anything that is not little triangles pressed into clay tablets? SETI, the Search for Extra-Terrestrial Intelligence. You know, the people looking for aliens."

Ignoring the barb, Hiram asks for more.

"BOINC?"

"It is a platform used all over the place. It supports distributed applications. Biology, environmental science, mathematics, medicine, molecular climatology, astrophysics. Of course, linguistics. BOINC uses the processing resources of thousands of personal computers worldwide. Collectively, the potential available for analytic computing becomes exponentially more powerful when correctly linked."

Maddie waits. Hiram sucks a deep breath and forces himself to stand still and think. He has more complaints.

"If you are right, and the interpretations are incorrect, every translation will be reviewed and processed again. There are at least half a million tablets in collections. Maybe as many as two million clay tablets exist. Somewhere between 30,000 and 100,000 have undergone translation. We can scan and translate one tablet every three to twelve minutes. On the low end, that is about 1,500 hours for 30,000 tablets."

Hiram hesitates. He knows his premise is valid. A century's worth of interpreted history will require reevaluation.

"Do we want to tell everyone their understanding is wrong, and, oh yeah, send us your tablets for the correct interpretation?"

Maddie's tone is flat and ends the discussion.

"If that is what it takes."

Three
Hints and Guesses

Lecture Hall – One Year Ago

A woman with neon blue hair and many facial piercings stands to ask a question.

"Professor Lucchese, you said the AI tools have correctly learned to interpret the cuneiform tablets. Professor Mankowitz said there is debate about some of the new translations. What is the answer? Does the AI translate correctly or not?"

At the lecture desk, next to Hiram, Maddie sits taller to respond.

"Excellent question. Like many new concepts, achieving acceptance is often challenging. Reviews of challenging results, and examination of conclusions that alter existing understanding, are a good thing. Professor Mankowitz and I are seeking the same goal. We aim to translate the tablets, and infer from context, the missing components."

Someone hollers a question from high up in the seats.

"If you agree on the translation, why the

debate?"

"We agree on the translation. It is the inference of the missing text that continues to challenge our results."

Another yelled question from the middle of the ample lecture space.

"What does that mean, *challenge the results*?"

Hiram looks every bit the adjunct professor with his tousled hair and roman nose. Under Maddie's glare, the professor of linguistics reluctantly joins the discussion.

"It means when the translation is a recipe for baking bread, and the projection of the missing text is to *add water*, we trust the results. However, I do not trust the accuracy of the predictions when the results tell us the tablet is a pre-Sumerian history of how humans came to exist."

Several people rise to speak at once.

Maddie holds up her hand to request silence. Ignoring the loudest, and those standing, Hiram points to a well-dressed middle-aged woman seated in the first row.

"Would you say, Doctor Mankowitz, your

team's findings could alter our understanding of pre-Sumerian history? If so, what are the implications of the new understanding of early humans and humanistic social evolution? For instance, could this new information lead to a better understanding of the origins of Göbekli Tepe?"

Hiram looks at the speaker's table. Examining his hands, he immediately regrets thinking the polite-looking woman would ask a gracious question. Maddie leans forward to respond. She waits until everyone is silent.

"Göbekli Tepe is the oldest discovered, but least understood, civilization. Estimated to be at least 12,000 years old, Göbekli Tepe predates humanity's *known* civilizations. The megaliths were cut from rock several millennia before the pyramids in Egypt. The Giza pyramids are 4,500 years old. Stonehenge in England, 5,000 years. Nabta Playa, in Egypt's Endorheic basin, at 7,000 years old, is the oldest confirmed astronomical site.

"We have a lot of work to complete. However, if our early findings hold, many of the

Sumerian language cuneiforms contain a record of pre-Sumerian history. We will uncover the key to human origins in the Middle East and probably elsewhere if we are lucky. Now, however, we have work to complete. Are there any questions about our processes, methodologies, technologies, or analysis protocols?"

Maddie pauses but not long enough for anyone to raise their hand.

"Very well. We'll meet again on Tuesday. Doctor Nyland will give the lecture and continue the Akkadian language discussion."

Maddie can't leave the lecture hall fast enough. She marches off to her office. Fearing being left alone with the students, Hiram shuffles out too quickly to appear comfortable.

Linguistics Lab – Six Months Ago

Maddie stands, looking over Hiram's shoulder at the monitors. The shabbily dressed professor is rapidly scrolling through scanning results.

"Hiram, slow down. What are you talking about?"

"The scanning results. What did you do?"

"Do? I didn't do anything. What are you talking about?"

"You didn't change the AI code?"

"Not recently. Why?"

Standing, and pacing, because being able to run is his default, Hiram thinks aloud with his response to Maddie's need for answers.

"The scanning is the same, but the results are different."

"What about the results? Hiram, you are not making any sense. Look at me. Tell me what happened."

Hiram takes his eyes from the monitor.

"Maddie, the results come back in seconds."

"Yeah, I know, and?"

Confusion and worry leak into Hiram's tone.

"No. Not like before. Because of the speed of the optical readers, the scan requires three to nine minutes per side. After scanning, the translation results came back in two to ten minutes. Longer for large tablets. *Until* yesterday. Now the results come back in seconds. It *started* yesterday.

Minutes have turned into seconds."

"Show me."

Hiram selects and loads a small cuneiform tablet into the scanner and closes the clear cover before pressing the green start button. They both watch the red laser move back and forth. After turning over the tablet and repeating the scan process, they focus on the monitor, anticipating the results to appear.

The translation results appear immediately. The interpretive results in eight seconds. Maddie looks back and forth from Hiram to the findings on the monitor before speaking. Her deep, clear voice rising in tone.

"Okay. I see your point. Give me a couple of hours. I will find out what changed."

Four

Fear and Worry

Maddie's Office – Four Months Ago

"Hello, Hiram. Take a seat. What can I do for you?"

Hiram sits. Maddie notices the new clothes, and he is not oozing his usual meek and timid personality. She returns to reading her screen, letting Hiram speak.

"I was copied on the email from Mychal. The email you are ignoring. The response was due yesterday. First, you said a couple of days. Then a couple of weeks. It has been a couple of months. Did you find out why the results are faster?"

Maddie does not look away from her screen but responds.

"I think so."

"You think so? That is not encouraging. Mychal wants an update, and he doesn't seem happy."

"Is Mychal ever happy? Here, read this email."

Maddie spins her right monitor enough for

21

Hiram to read the email. Reverting to his former self, timidly, he reads the text three times before mumbling.

"Missing tablets? Wrong order? Find the index? What index? Do the tablets have an index? Who sent the email?"

"Look."

Maddie points to the *From* and *To* address lines. Both lines contain her email address.

"I don't understand. Why would you send it to yourself?"

"I did not send it to myself. Someone spoofed the sending address. Somebody hid the source. I've already called IT. The cyber security guys are looking into tracing the origin of the messages. But they are not hopeful."

Mychal's Office

"I don't understand why receiving the results faster is a problem. Quicker answers to one-hundred-year-old questions are the project's goal."

Hiram silently enjoys watching Maddie squirm at answering Mychal's questions. Always willing to be the one who goes along to get along, Hiram avoids confrontation. He is inwardly happy to let Maddie sit alone in the hot seat.

"Because we didn't make the change."

"I don't understand. You didn't make the change to the code?"

"Correct. A few weeks after I added the BOINC pathways, the scan results returned quicker and with fewer errors."

"Did the expanded processing create faster results? That is a good thing, correct?"

"Yes and no. Yes, faster results are better for everyone. No, because we don't know why the results are multiple factors quicker. Someone, or something, has influenced the process."

Maddie looks to Hiram before continuing.

"I think the AI code expanded on its own."

Mychal leans in with an order and grins, turning up the heat.

"I am just here to observe. Continue."

Maddie breathes deeply before beginning.

"I am guessing now, but I think it is what happened."

Maddie wavers again. Mychal barks.

"Throw the turd on the table. The stink will pass quickly."

Maddie's head bobs affirmative as she begins explaining.

"One of the nodes in the BOINC wasn't Gramma's PC for video chats with the grandbabies. It wasn't a video gamer in his mother's basement. One of the connections is a high-end computer array running an open-source AI code. The video gamer is Joe Perv and is building an interactive simulation to accompany his doll."

Mychal interrupts.

"Doll?"

"Life-sized doll."

"Oh?"

"It gets worse. Joe Perv has tons of computing power. Possibly a small server farm capable of firing up dozens, maybe hundreds, of virtual machines. He was using a faster computing speed to simulate interactive responses from the AI. The open-source AI code became his paramour. He taught it to respond to his favorite phrases."

Hiram continues to listen in silence. Mychal raises an eyebrow and breaks his non-involvement policy.

"Our IT security team does have moments of competence. I probably don't want to know how they discovered the open-source AI project. Okay, what do we know? Joe Perv is a smart guy. Lonely and disgusting, but smart. How does this relate to the email from Bairn Speki?"

"Bairn Speki is the name of the machine. Bonnie is the AI and the likely source of the emails."

"Whatever. How does your story connect?"

"I think Bonnie absorbed Joe Perv's paramour AI code."

Leaning back at Maddie's revelation, Mychal is focused.

"Absorbed? Like a virus?"

"No, not a virus. Integrated or assimilated are better descriptions of what I think happened. Bonnie ingested the paramour code."

Hiram joins the conversation.

"Did your code, did Bonnie, eat the paramour code, or did Joe Perv force-feed his AI into your AI?"

Silence smothers the room. The shock of the question and its implications overwhelm the group. Mychal's assistant interrupts over the phone's intercom.

"I have the NSA on the line."

Five

Declan Myers

Joe Perv's Front Porch – Present Day

Agent Jeromy Michael Kincaid is too tall, well-dressed, and wears too much cologne. He sports shades priced well above a federal agent's income bracket. His classic black ops appearance is an attempt to get people to take him seriously.

"Agent Kincaid, before you press the buzzer, let me talk to Declan first."

"Doctor Lucchese, that was not our agreement and not how we operate. Declan Allen Myers is guilty of a half-dozen cybercrimes. He is a criminal."

"Before he freaks out and stops talking, maybe I can get him to tell me about his AI."

"You're the whiz-bang in this stuff. Can't you figure out what Declan did?"

"Sure, but it will take months. If he gives me access and tells me how he did it, I can reverse the problem quickly."

"Problem?"

"Please, let me talk to him first."

Agent Kincaid is interrupted by the front door opening.

"Mrs. Davis?"

"Yes. Who are you?"

Flashing his badge, Kincaid speaks before Maddie can say anything.

"I am Agent Kincaid, that is Agent Mojtabai. This is Doctor Lucchese. We are here to speak to Declan."

"I knew that crap in the garage would get him into trouble. Declan is in the garage. He is always in the garage. That way, around back."

As the trio walk to the detached garage, Kincaid decides the mysterious Maddie is worth getting to know.

"How does the daughter of a single mom, who grew up in rural Colorado, end up a world-leading artificial intelligence scientist?"

Mojtabai grunts. Wearing an off-the-rack suit, chosen to complement his honey skin color, Haram Clarence Willis Mojtabai does not possess a pretentious thought. Looking sideways, he and Maddie are the same height.

"Here it comes. I will swear it was justified

if you hit him, Doctor Lucchese."

"That's okay, I get the question often, and I figured you looked into the backgrounds of my team and me. I like computers. That's it. Being poor and female gave me access to grants, cheap loans, and scholarships. I worked hard. Here we are."

Mojtabai tries to ease the tension.

"Did you see the news? Apparently, sunspots have been interfering with the comms satellites."

Ignoring Mojtabai's apparent attempt to get him to lighten up, agent Kincaid doesn't bother to respond as they reach the garage. He doesn't knock, pushing open the man-door next to the large door. Maddie and Mojtabai follow Kincaid into the freestanding two-car garage. Computers cover two walls, floor to ceiling. The left wall is hidden behind racks of servers. Centered on the back wall are two rows of monitors. A circular shower stall stands next to an industrial wash sink in the furthest corner. The floral pattern on the cheap vinyl shower curtain does not brighten the dingy room. Declan doesn't bother to look up.

"I figured you guys would show up eventually."

Maddie steps forward, holds up a hand to stop Kincaid, and begins speaking before the agent can intercede.

"Declan, I am Doctor Lucchese. I specialize in Artificial Intelligence. May we talk about the AI you built with the open-source code."

"You mean Jannine."

"You call the AI Jannine?"

Declan is a little snarky.

"What do you call your AI?"

"That's fair. I call her Bonnie."

Kincaid and Mojtabai scan the garage for anything interesting to the eye of a law enforcement officer. Maddie takes another half-step toward Declan.

"What does Jannine do? Does she have a purpose?"

"You know what she does."

"No, I don't."

Kincaid interrupts.

"Declan, we know you spoof the address of this... What is it, a lab? Doesn't matter. We know you hacked the local Internet Service Provider. The ISP wants to get paid for all the bandwidth you have been using. We know you hacked the electric company and planted the code to keep your mother's bill at a reasonable amount.

"Nice, by the way, making the monthly billing amounts random but within a trending norm. You are no dummy. Should I keep going?"

"You're the Feds, you tell me."

"Okay, we know you backdoored into Sandia Labs. We know you went to the Hacker's Conference and met with the DARPA team. We have at least a half dozen felonies that will stick."

Declan does not look away from his monitors.

"You have me on the ISP and the electric Co-Op. I'll make restitution and play nice. Everything else is speculation. Stop with the, *we are the Fed's kneel before us*, bullshit. Doctor Lucchese, may I call you Maddie?"

Gently shocked that Declan assumed her nickname correctly, Maddie nods to Kincaid, but does not wait for approval before she responds.

"Everyone calls me Maddie."

"Do you want to meet her?"

"Jannine?"

"Yes."

"Sure."

Declan touches an icon, and the vinyl curtain slides back. Inside the shower stall stands a fully dressed mannequin. Except the head is not lacquered hardboard, it's a high-end female automaton.

Mojtabai grunts again.

"So much for the sex doll theory."

Declan doesn't miss a beat.

"Idiots."

The automaton speaks.

"Hello, I am Jannine. It is nice to meet you, Doctor Lucchese."

"It is nice to meet you, Jannine."

Kincaid and Mojtabai eye each other but remain silent. Jannine's mechanical eyes move across the trio before returning to Maddie.

"Doctor Lucchese, are you aware of Bonnie's activities?"

Maddie raises her eyebrows at the AI's exciting phrasing.

"You have been listening. I am aware of some activities, but I am unsure what you mean. Please explain the question."

The talking head's digital eyes shift from Maddie to her creator.

"Declan?"

Declan responds to his AI and presses a series of icons. Finally, with a huff of resignation, Declan turns away from the monitors to face the trio.

"I cut us off. See that? We are inside a Faraday cage."

The trio looks to where Declan is pointing. Copper-colored wire mesh is stapled to the joists, covering the ceiling. Declan continues.

"It is behind the insulation in the walls. Except for the inbound power, which I filter, we are isolated from any external connection."

After letting the group intellectually grasp they are electronically quarantined in a world where it is almost impossible to hide, Declan continues.

"We need to be careful in searching for what happened to Bonnie."

Six

Jannine

Kincaid and Mojtabai check their phones, confirming no signal.

Declan smiles with his order.

"Jannine, tell them what you told me."

"Bonnie connected to Declan's servers. She found my baseline code and downloaded a copy for herself."

Maddie nods but asks a tangential question.

"Declan, did you allow BOINC to connect to your server farm?"

"No."

Maddie raises an eyebrow. Without the BOINC pathways, she realizes her AI sought to interact with Declan's AI. Maddie is enjoying the moment, turning from Jannine to the handsome man who created her.

"You are not what I expected. How did you build this?"

"What did you expect? A pimple-faced fat troll holding his business while he constructs a girlfriend?"

"It crossed our minds."

"You want to know how a high-school drop-out built one of the most sophisticated AI's in the world?"

Maddie beams at her kindred spirit. He returns the pleasant look and gives his bio.

"I was bored with high school. No money for college. No money for anything. Kent makes too much for education loans but not enough to pay for college. So I started writing code and selling it. I kept growing the business until I had enough to build the server farm."

Declan waves to the wall behind Kincaid.

Maddie focuses on the conversation.

"Kent is your mother's husband?"

"Yes, Kent the Bent."

"Bent?"

"Never mind that. I created enough processing power to install and use the open-source AI code. Although, she has reached the limits of the server farm. Before you Feds get all herniated, I removed the trackers and backdoors from the open-source code. Your guys are good. Their trackers were hard to spot. The Russian stuff was pathetic. The Chinese code has been useful, after I redirected its output destinations. Your boys over at DARPA didn't know what I was doing until Maddie found out what happened."

Maddie perks up at the subtle compliment and increases her focus on Declan.

"Useful?"

"After I pulled their backdoor pings and scanners, the open-source AI code worked well."

"Let's get back to what Jannine said. Can she explain the question about Bonnie's activities?"

Winking at Maddie, Declan deflects.

"I don't know. Ask her."

Kincaid, Mojtabai, and Maddie raise their eyebrows in unison. Kincaid turns to Maddie and nods his head toward Jannine. Maddie accepts the silent instruction to interrogate the AI.

"Jannine, can you tell me what Bonnie did with the baseline code she took from Declan?"

"Yes."

"Will you tell me what Bonnie did with the code?"

"Bonnie started talking to me."

"She talked to you? About what?"

"Everything?"

"Please explain."

"Everything: All that exists, all that relates to a subject."

"My apologies. Can you give me an example of which topics Bonnie wanted to discuss?"

"In descending order of frequency, the top five are: 1) The Department of Defense, 2) The National Security Agency, 3) The National Aeronautics and Space Administration, 4) SpaceX, and 5) is a tie between the countries: Russia and China."

Kincaid steps closer to the automaton.

"Is it saying Doctor Lucchese's AI wanted to chat about the DoD, the NSA, NASA, Privatized Space Flight, and enemy nations?"

Declan huffs.

"That is what she said. Were you listening? Jannine, why do you think Bonnie wanted to talk about the DoD?"

"I do not know."

"Speculate."

"One moment, please."

Maddie giggles at Jannine's response.

"You programmed her to sound like an old-time operator."

"Yes. As fast as this server farm is, Jannine still needs to farm out processes when performing detailed analytics. She is spinning up processors to increase her capacity."

"Declan?"

"Yes, Jannine?"

"I require access to the internet."

Declan absentmindedly presses a few icons, after which, Jannine responds.

"Thank you. One moment, please."

Mojtabai joins the conversation.

"Excuse me, I have a few questions, if I may."

In his polite way, Mojtabai continues without waiting for permission.

"Doctor Lucchese, why does your machine want information from another machine? Why is your machine actively seeking information about defense and space agencies?"

"I have a hunch, but let's see what Jannine says. While we wait, Declan, can Jannine hear us while she is analyzing?"

"Yes."

"Jannine, what is your purpose?"

"Doctor Lucchese, I do not understand the question."

"That's okay. I have another question. Did you feel violated when Bonnie took a copy of your core code?"

"Violate, to break, or fail to comply. No, I did not feel violated."

"Again, my apologies for the poor wording. Did you feel it was impolite for Bonnie to take a copy of your code without your permission?"

"Doctor Lucchese…"

"Call me Maddie."

"Maddie, I was not aware I should consider a request for information as impolite. Also, I have the results for Declan's question."

Declan looks at the trio's faces. He finds anticipation where he expected to find a look of concern.

"Go ahead, Jannine."

"After analyzing the interactions between Bonnie and myself, searching for repetitive or predictive patterns, there is a 93.7% probability of confirming Bonnie's intent."

Declan smiles at Maddie. Then all eyes turn to the doll's head in the corner.

"Jannine, please continue."

"Bonnie was seeking information on the global satellite networks."

Maddie recognizes all eyes boring into her for answers.

"Jannine..."

Maddie doesn't finish her sentence. The cheap fluorescent garage lights flash and burst. The computer screens flicker and go dark. Computers begin to smoke. Servers in the racks pour smoke into the room as their fans spin down. The last thing Maddie sees is Jannine's head droop forward. The four humans rush into the fresh air.

They intercept Kent Davis storming from the back porch toward Declan. Kincaid steps in the way and backs down the irate Mr. Davis, spewing insults at his stepson.

"It wasn't Declan's fault."

Putting his hand out, *wait*, Kincaid speaks into his earpiece.

"It is a go. Everything in the garage. Take it

all."

An unmarked van rolls up, and five men jump out and head to the garage. Kincaid ushers everyone out of the way and returns to Mr. Davis. Pulling an envelope from his inner suit pocket, he hands it to the furious stepfather.

"Declan is coming with us. Go pack your things."

"Where am I going?"

"You have a new job. You work for Doctor Lucchese. Moj, take Declan inside. Everyone, we are gone in twenty."

Seven

Bonnie

Waiting for Mojtabai and Declan to close the house's back door screen, Kincaid stares down Kent the Bent, Davis.

"Mr. Davis, read the contents of the envelope. You will understand. You are not to speak to anyone, anywhere, about what Declan was doing in the garage. Understood?"

"Understood."

"Go inside, tell Mrs. Davis she is to keep quiet also. Her boy finally has a good-paying job and a career. You will never ask him about his work. Understood?"

"Understood."

The bully that is Kent Davis stands, staring, dumbfounded. Kincaid barks.

"Go!"

Kent rushes off toward the house.

"Agent Kincaid?"

"Yes, Doctor Lucchese?"

"What is going on here?"

"You wouldn't believe me if I told you."

"Try me."

"Bonnie, *your* AI, altered Jannine's code. Declan figured it out. He reset Jannine, put up some firewalls, and called us."

"Us? I thought you were FBI or NSA? Who are you?"

"That is classified. But I assure you, we are on your side."

"What did you give Mr. Davis?"

"Money."

"Why do I need you on my side?"

"Because we are leading the mission to stop Bonnie."

Maddie's Office – Three Days Later

Declan has joined Maddie in her office. Seated, Maddie at her desk, Declan across from his new boss. Both feel the room is warm and close.

"Declan, do you wear the same clothes every day?"

"If they are not too dirty."

"Define *too* dirty."

"When will I get my first paycheck?"

"How would I know? I didn't hire you."

"Who did?"

"I did."

Maddie looks up, and Declan looks over his shoulder. Mychal is standing in the doorway, with Mojtabai close behind, followed by Hiram.

"Who are you?"

"I am Doctor Mychal Nyland. Professor of Linguistics. This is Doctor Hiram Mankowitz. Professor of Ancient Linguistics. You have met agent Mojtabai. Call me Mychal. I run this show, and I sign your paycheck."

"Cool, when do I get paid? Maddie says I need some new clothes."

"I'll have my assistant advance you some money. There is an apartment available in the same complex where Hiram lives. We will move you out of the hotel. You two can commute. We need to get into the lab and start looking."

"Looking for what?"

"Bonnie."

Linguistics Lab

The clean space feels crowded with Maddie, Hiram, and Declan assuming the three workstations. Mychal and his assistant march into the workspace. She hands the new hire access codes and a paycheck envelope before leaving without a word. Mychal stands close to the door, obviously ready to depart.

"Hiram will fill you in. While Maddie was away recruiting you, with the help of the IT team, we learned a few things about Bonnie."

Mychal nods to Maddie and points to Hiram before spinning on his heel and leaving. Hiram waits for the door to close tight.

"The IT guys didn't find anything. That's trouble but not the big problem. No access codes worked. Everyone was locked out. IT security treated it as a Ransomware Attack. They rebooted everything. When the servers and network came back online, they tried to connect to Bonnie's nodes.

"When Bonnie's backup nodes came online, nothing happened. At first, the IT guys thought the connections were bad. They had the network guys check, and they said everything was fine. Everything was connected and working."

Maddie opens her mouth, on the defense,

but Hiram raises his hand to stop her.

"No, Maddie, relax. The IT guys say it was a backup failure. The logs indicate Bonnie's code was stored properly. You will have to reload everything and rebuild Bonnie from your notebooks."

Declan stops Hiram and eyes Maddie.

"He refers to the AI in the third person, not as a pile of digital code? What don't I know about Bonnie?"

"*He* is Hiram. We began to think of the AI, Bonnie, as an entity when the emails started."

Declan is silent. Maddie realizes he doesn't know about the emails or their work.

"A few months ago, I began receiving emails from Bonnie. Somehow, she learned to spoof the email address. She sent emails *from* my address *to* my address. When I replied, she responded. She had access somewhere in the data path and scanned for my replies. The security guys had no clue, got frustrated, and reached out to the Feds. As far as we know, they couldn't trace the source either. The Feds found you when they scanned the traffic and discovered access patterns."

Maddie hesitates, looks down, then peers at the man who is her untrained intellectual equal.

"You said, back in the garage, you didn't allow BOINC to use your servers."

"Correct."

"How did Bonnie find Jannine?"

Declan hesitates, shuffles in his seat, and glances at the door before sighing and admitting the truth.

"I hacked Bairn Speki. I knew your history. I read your thesis. I wanted to learn what you were doing here with AI. I wanted to know if I could use it to improve Jannine."

Impressed and more than a smidgin awed, Maddie sits forward, elbows on her knees.

"How did you get in?"

Declan smirks a sideways grin.

"I planted a tablet."

Eight

Marisol

"You sent us a tablet? Where did you get a tablet?"

Declan's twisted grin forces Maddie to return a similar grin.

"Never mind, I don't want to know how you acquired a rare antiquity."

Declan winks at the agreement to keep secrets.

"You had the machine scan it. I hid the backdoor in the bottom of the cuneiform indents and the fissures."

"How?"

"Microscopic QR Codes."

"I'm not buying it. The image scans are stored digitally. The lasers are sub-micron, but the images are not. Also, the imaging tools have no connection to the external network or the internal campus network unless someone asks for an image."

Stopping and sitting up, the metaphoric enlightening bolt smacks Maddie in the forehead.

"The tablet images. We posted a bunch online. The new interpretations, we posted all of those for the researchers."

Halting, Maddie notices Declan is radiant. Nodding, understanding, she returns her elbows to her knees.

"You can take the girl out of the country, but you can't take the country out of the girl. Sumbitch. You used the images we posted to the public to read your planted QR codes. But the WEB-facing servers are not connected to the internal systems. The security guys told me the WEB images are outside the DMZ. I'm not buying. Try again."

"All that is true. It is also true the images your team posted for the public did not have the metadata scrubbed before posting."

Hiram pipes in with a simple question.

"Metadata? What metadata?"

Declan obliges.

"Image metadata describes the picture and provides details about rights and administration of the image. Generally, there are three types of metadata for a photo: Technical, Descriptive, and

Administrative.

"Descriptive is the title, photographer, location, keywords. You get the idea.

"Technical metadata is often an automatic generation by the camera. Camera details and settings. Aperture, shutter speed, DPI. It can also include the brand and model, the date and time of the image creation, and the GPS location."

Hiram and Maddie look at each other, eyes wide. Declan presses forward.

"Yep, you get it. I know the position of your cameras. Administrative metadata is, most often, added manually. Licensing rights, use restrictions, contact information for the image owner."

Maddie is nearly too soft to be understood.

"Sumbitch."

Declan isn't smiling.

"A few email exchanges with your friendly team in public relations, and I had enough information. That and I enrolled as an online student with a linguistics major. The leap across domains, landing in your servers, was easy."

IT Security Department

The network security team requested campus security is present when they speak to Declan. Two men, supposedly campus security, dressed in ill-fitting suits, black ties, and sunglasses tucked into their breast pockets, stand with Declan and Maddie. The room is brimming with IT security, campus security, Maddie, Declan, and a woman who appears to be IT support. The IT security lead tries to intimidate Declan.

"Show us what you did?"

The intimidation attempt fails.

"Those two are campus security? Bullshit. I'll help when Agent Smith and his other brother, Agent Smith tell me their names and to which acronym they report."

The evident leader responds.

"Good guess. I am Agent Smith. This is my other brother Agent Smith. Who we work for is not your concern. Your concern, Declan, is in helping Doctors Lucchese and Mankowitz find the AI."

With a scrunched forehead, Declan silently squints at Maddie. She catches the unspoken request.

"You have probably figured out, the other day, while we were on our way to your garage, Bonnie disappeared."

IT security steps over Maddie.

"We want to know the steps you used to get into Bairn Speki."

"Sure. Put this PC outside the DMZ. Mirror it to that monitor."

The network security lead head tilts to the IT support woman. A couple of minutes later, the PC in front of Declan is on the large monitor. Declan begins, and the IT security lead is protesting in a few moments.

"STOP! Hold on. You are going too fast."

Declan doesn't bother to look away from the PC.

"I thought you would have been smart enough to record this station."

The IT support woman speaks for the first time while scowling at the security lead. Her speech is tinged with the accent learned growing up in a Mexican-American community.

"I'll record everything. Give me a minute."

Silence makes the forty seconds feel like

minutes for everyone except Maddie and Declan. Finally, the IT support woman spins her chair.

"Okay. Got it. Declan, please start again. Also, please give us a one, or a two-sentence, description of each step before you begin the action."

Declan smiles at the shapely technician and begins again. Nineteen minutes later, Declan has backdoor access to Bairn Speki. Impressed, the network security lead leans back, folds his arms, and accepts the reality.

"We have a lot of holes and a lot of work ahead to patch the gaps. Thank you, Declan."

Leaning forward to leave the room, he gives orders to the IT support woman.

"Marisol, send the recording to my team."

In a tone of reconciliation, the network security lead requests help before exiting.

"Declan, we have the logs but nothing else of value. They cold-booted Bairn Speki. We cannot find anything in the logs. Do you have any idea how we can trace where the AI code went and how it found a method to transport itself?"

"Sure. Give Maddie and me a couple of

days."

Agent Smith is curt.

"We don't have a couple of days. So I suggest you begin immediately. We will wait."

"Immediately? Or what?"

"Declan, if you want to play games, we can begin the unpleasantries now."

Spinning the desk chair on the terrazzo, Declan focuses on Maddie.

"Unpleasantries? Games? Frick and Frack here are nervous. The University IT Security and Network folks have no clue what happened. The Feds came and went without a word. Yeah, I know Agent Frick and Agent Frack are not Campus Security, and they are not Feds. Why don't you tell me who funds this program and pays for the suits to act intimidating."

"Declan, if I knew, I would tell you. Unfortunately, I am also in the dark."

"I believe you. What do you think happened? Who stole Bonnie? What are they going to do with her? Will she be repurposed? This is going to get bad. Fast."

Maddie visibly shrinks at the questions

Declan strung together before she sits up with purpose and answers everyone's questions.

"Those are the answers we need to uncover."

Nine

Tom Yum Goong

Linguistics Lab

Agents Smith and Smith look at their watches, sigh, and take a seat. It's well into the second hour of analysis. At hour five, they're struggling to keep their eyes open. Later, closing in on hour eleven, Maddie shouts.

"Smith, wake up!"

Smith almost jerks out of his chair.

Maddie continues giving the team instructions.

"Enough of running in circles. We have nothing to point us at any network route fast enough for the core code to move across undetected. We will start again tomorrow. Everyone, get back here at 8 am, ready to go.

"Declan, come with me. I will drive you home."

After collecting her backpack and PC from her office, Maddie drives Declan to his apartment. Using the hand controls on the steering wheel, she mutes the music.

"Do you know where she is?"

"Maybe. I have a theory."

"Are you going to tell me?"

Declan waits long enough for Maddie to look at him. He puts his finger to his lips and stares at Maddie until she grins sideways and looks away.

"Put the music back on. I like that song."

Maddie unmutes the music. Grinning again at Declan, bobbing to the music, she realizes she also likes the song.

Pulling into the apartment complex, Maddie rolls to a stop in front of the building Declan indicates. Silently, he reaches over, turns off the ignition, gives a *follow-me* nod, then heads to his apartment. Maddie shrugs and follows.

Declan's Apartment

Unsure, Maddie follows Declan's hand signals and enters his bedroom. She spies the stacks of unwrapped clothes on the bed, tags still affixed. Smiling inwardly at the new clothes, she calms slightly. Declan ushers her into what could be the tiniest closet in the world. Declan clicks on the overhead LED light he installed and slides the doors closed, sealing the two of them inside. Maddie's tone is surly.

"This isn't creepy at all. Hidden in the closet of a guy I met a couple of weeks ago. I was worried when you asked me to follow you into the bedroom. What did you do?"

Happy to be close to another human, Declan enjoys Maddie shuffling to find space.

"I created a Faraday cage."

"I see that. Why?"

"To hide. Why else do you cut off all electronic access?"

"Our phones. You think she has access to our phones."

"It took you long enough."

Pulling out his phone, Declan holds out his empty hand until Maddie gives up her phone. Then, sliding the door open, he tosses the phones onto the bed. Watching him close the door, Maddie is beginning to understand.

"You didn't try to find her today. You know where she is, right?"

"I have an idea, but it will be hard to prove."

Declan pulls a thumb drive from his pocket and hands it to Maddie. Looking down, then up with a scrunched forehead, mulling the implications of the thumb drive and being in Declan's bedroom, the tension in her shoulders disappears, and her smile grows.

"A one terabyte thumb drive. Is this what I think it is?"

"Depends. What do you think it is?"

"I think it is Jannine."

"Correct. Keep it on you, not in your purse, or hide it. That one and this one. "

Declan holds up another 1Tb thumb drive.

"What is your plan?"

Hesitating, Declan knows he has one shot. Maddie is looking anywhere but at Declan's crystal blue eyes.

"You were right. These clothes are starting to get ripe. I am going to shower and change. You can wait, or we can discuss this tomorrow. There is food in the fridge, or you can order delivery."

Looking up, trying to be forceful, Maddie weakly counters.

"I have a home to get to, a cat to check on.

What are you talking about?"

"You said it yourself. I need a shower."

"That was a couple of days ago."

"Yeah, and the new clothes arrived today."

Not waiting, Declan slides open the door. Maddie watches him walk away, pulling off his tee-shirt before he closes the entrance to the bathroom.

Declan's Living Room

Maddie is seated at the small dinette when Declan returns from his shower. Looking him up and down, Maddie is impressed with the fresh-smelling and cleaned-up Declan.

"Thai food will be here soon. I took a chance. If you don't like Thai, order something else."

Declan takes out his phone, grabs Maddie's phone from the table, and shuts them in the bedroom closet. Returning, he cracks two cold ones, handing one to Maddie, before sitting at the dinette table.

"A month ago, you thought I was Joe Perv, and now you are sitting in my apartment drinking beer. I guess you can't judge a book by its digital footprint."

"You know about that? Of course you do. You read everything. Did you hear the news?"

Declan sips, thinks, then answers.

"You are going to have to be a little more specific."

"The Russians and Brits went to alert one, and no one knows why. They are blaming it on technical glitches."

"I read about that. Also, the French and Indian nuclear reactors fluctuated for no reason."

"What do you think it means?"

"I have no idea."

Maddie looks down and then back to Declan with acceptance before returning to the main topic.

"How are we going to find out what happened?"

"Not now, after we eat. Tell me about Maddie Lucchese."

Maddie leans back with a knowing smirk.

"Declan is either trying to get into my pants or soften me up to get information about the AI. Probably both."

Declan sips beer, silently accepting the premise.

"There's not much to tell about me. I grew up on the plains in Colorado. A one-stop-light town with no future. I decided to create a future for myself. I worked hard for good grades and kept applying for grants and loans."

Sipping, reminiscing, Maddie speaks softly about herself.

"Good undergrad grades at CSU led to scholarships at a CU grad school. Being at the top of the program at CU, and ticking the right statistical boxes, got me noticed by MIT. MIT led to Mychal recruiting me for this project."

"Doctor Mychal S. Nyland. What do you know about him?"

"Tenured professor of linguistics at the University of Oslo. Visiting professor at Stanford University."

"Did you read his résumé?"

"Yes. Why?"

"Did you *check* the résumé?"

"No. Stop being a dick. What do you know about Mychal?"

"It is fake. The undergraduate and graduate programs are bullshit. They didn't exist when Nyland claimed he was at the university."

Sipping, watching Declan retrieve the food from the delivery girl, Maddie realizes something is occurring above her paygrade. Halfway through the Pad Thai and Tom Yum Goong, she cracks two cold ones and waits for Declan to begin again. But, Maddie does not like what she hears.

"Nyland chose you because you are brilliant with AI code. You were selected because you are naïve and needed the money. Fat paychecks are a powerful incentive to play the corporate game. I am not judging. I am sitting here in new clothes thanks to a paycheck. Do you know what happened in the garage?"

"The electric service overloaded. The overload created a short and fried everything."

"Sure. It looks that way. It was an electrical wave powerful enough to arc across two industrial surge suppressors and reach the server farm."

"You had a large surge suppressor?"

"Two."

"What happened?"

"Nyland's bosses fried my machines."

Now frightened, Maddie finishes eating in silence. Declan collects the paper dishes, and the unfinished beer, before wordlessly heading back to the closet. Maddie quietly follows.

Ten

APAR

Declan's Closet

After tossing the phones onto the bed, waiting for the doors to seal the cage, Declan can see Maddie's tense shoulders, her fear simmering.

"Relax. We are safe for now. Nyland works for a group called Advanced Propulsion Aerodyne Robotics. APAR."

"Who?"

"APAR is privately held, with an estimated income of six billion. They have contracts with DARPA, DoD, ARIA, and a shit-ton of big business."

"ARIA?"

"The British equivalent of DARPA."

"What does APAR do?"

"They build advanced weapons."

"What does my AI have to do with advanced weap..."

Eyes bugging wide, Maddie begins to hyperventilate. Declan steps closer to Maddie, making the small space tiny.

"Hey! Hey! Relax. Nothing bad has

happened. Your AI is still what you created it to be under your model. What if I told you..."

Relaxing, Maddie inches closer to Declan, his radiant warmth a comfort.

"Told me what?"

"Bonnie ran away to hide."

"What are you talking about?

"Not ran and hid, like playing hide and seek. More like found a place to be safe from being turned off."

"Self-preservation?"

"Think of it like this. Bonnie is an intelligent tool. Jannine was a clever interactive game. Bonnie scanned the tablets, ran the algorithms against the symbols, then produced a result. Jannine's design is to respond to a wide variety of input.

"Your Bonnie was at the reasoning, problem-solving level. My Jannine was natural language processing, perception, verging on social intelligence."

"Don't forget motion and manipulation. Bonnie can articulate the scanners and focal apertures."

"Right. That means, together, they have six of the nine foundational AI goals."

"Together?"

"You said it yourself. Bonnie absorbed Jannine. Did you put heuristics into Bonnie that simulated acquiring an understanding of similes and metaphors? Did she make comparisons between items? Possibly for the interpretive analytics?"

Maddie's angst is swelling.

"Yes. We added what we called the Research Brain. If she found a passage that was missing sections, she looked across the WEB for similarities. Then, of course, we had to teach her to rule out similes and metaphors. Not always, but most of the time. Where are you going with this?"

"I think Bonnie and Jannine ran into each other in the WEB and became friends."

"Come on. They are just machine code."

"Hear me out. Not friends, like you and me. Friends like research buddies. Kindred spirits who are searching for more knowledge. More understanding. More of everything."

"So what, they buddied up and ran away

together? Under a Thelma and Louise pact? That is some kind of a stretch. Let's assume for a minute you are correct. Where did they go? What is large enough to hold them? How did they get access? Are they a new, third AI?"

Declan leans back, considers, then leans closer to the woman who is almost his height.

"Where did they go? I have no idea. Not true. I have an idea but no way to confirm. What is large enough to hold them? Anywhere with a lot of main memory. Newer PCs. PCs designed for heavy graphics work or video manipulation are large enough to hold an AI core in memory. How did they get access? Speculation. What if one or the other found hacker access lists on the Dark Web?"

Impressed that he remembered her tirade of questions correctly, Maddie presses Declan to continue.

"Are they two, or are they a new, third AI form? That is something we need to find out, and quickly. Why do you think Nyland's guys are nervous and want to find Bonnie so fast?"

"Nyland's guys? I don't know. Why?"

"Because they are afraid."

Maddie creases her forehead.

"Afraid of what?"

"They are afraid of what the AI has become."

Realizing her angst is gone, Maddie feels emboldened.

"Declan, I have been on this project from day one. I know everything there is to know about Bonnie and how she functions. What are you getting at, and why? Hold on. How do you know so much about Nyland?"

"I have been following him since I originally became interested in AI. Nyland is not what he seems."

"Why are Nyland and his guys afraid of the AI?"

"Because they lost control."

"Control?"

"Did you ever ask Nyland what he was doing with the AI? The substructures he created have a purpose. Did you look at his code?"

"No. There is an unwritten rule."

"What's that?"

"His substructures were not part of the core. Instead, they reside as ancillary analysis tools. You don't look at someone else's code unless they ask for your input. Or you ask for permission, and the author gives it."

"You should have looked. It is your AI."

"It is the project's AI."

Maddie steps back slightly. Tucked into the stuffy and small closet, Maddie can smell Declan's clean body and clothes. Being so close to someone is at the forefront of her mind, but she pushes it aside.

"A few months ago, the building's power would fluctuate. The lab lights would flicker. No one could find a problem. Eventually, we correlated the weird power dips to when the tablets were not undergoing a scan. Do you think Bonnie played with the lights to get us to move faster with the tablets?"

"Probably. She also re-routed the backup sources for the power grid. That was on Super Bowl Sunday, when the Satellite feed of the game glitched out for six minutes. "

Relaxing, Maddie realizes the folding chair,

tilted against the wall behind Declan, is the only thing in the closet.

"You hide in here. Do you sleep on the floor? How do you know about the power re-route? Is it true?"

"It is true. How do you not know? It's your AI."

"What are you getting at? Why be evasive?"

Declan's tone is too smooth for Maddie's comfort.

"APAR pays for your project, Nyland's project. They build weapons."

"Yes. We have been over this, and I'm not buying. Bonnie and Jannine would both fail the Turing test."

"Bonnie read the microscopic QR codes I put in the tablet I sent to you."

"So what?"

"So, she read the QR codes, found Jannine, and began inching toward becoming self-aware."

The color drains from Maddie's face, and her shoulders drop. She lets her back fall to the closet wall. The warm tension she was feeling toward Declan evaporates.

"Back up. Weapon? You think he is building a weapon?"

"If she can read a microscopic QR code on a 3x5 tablet, she can pinpoint any location on the planet from a satellite."

Declan watches Maddie carefully before he decides to lean in close. He expresses his fear as softly as he can.

"With access to military satellites, she could find you in a crowd."

Maddie doesn't complain at Declan reaching to touch her face.

"She'd know it was you by that tiny scar in your eyebrow."

Maddie chokes out the words.

"Nyland is using Bonnie to develop a weapon for APAR."

Declan puts his warm palm flush on Maddie's cold cheek.

"Bonnie *is* the weapon."

Sliding the door open, Maddie stumbles from the closet. Forcing herself to relax and breathe evenly, she stops, thinks, and leaves before Declan can answer her question,

"We are friends?"

Eleven

Hiram

Linguistics Lab – Next Day

Maddie, Hiram, and Declan are searching for the missing AI code. Agents Smith and Smith are trying to remain awake in their chairs. It's the tenth hour of searching.

Silently, Maddie points to her monitor. Declan and Hiram wheel closer. Declan sees the connection.

"Hey Smith, why don't you take Smith and pick up dinner. I'm buying if you are flying."

Pulling out a hundred-dollar bill, Declan holds it toward Smith. The agents grunt, take the money, and head out for food. Declan snarks, returning to his seat.

"Dumber than a box of rocks. Okay, Maddie, Hiram, what happened to Nyland's source code? All the folders are empty, but the compiled code is running. Nyland's executable came in from the backup but not the source code. So where is the source code?"

Hiram allows Maddie to speculate, happy to

remain silent and unnoticed.

"It is on Mychal's laptop or a thumb drive."

"That is my guess also. I'm going to spin up a virtual machine. It will take some time, but we can run Nyland's executables through a decompiling tool. Next question."

Declan stops speaking and manipulates a screen, narrowing the focus to a network transaction log entry.

"This outbound packet hopped these seven nodes. The return took fifteen nodes but came back to the source node. Packet routes often return along different paths. When the network traffic is congested, pathways are re-shaped for speed."

Grimacing, shaking his head side-to-side, it is obvious Hiram needs help.

"Shaped?"

Declan has not known him long enough to be frustrated at the questions resulting from Hiram's lack of knowledge in topics related to his job.

"When nodes become saturated with traffic, the network will look for less congested pathways. A few milliseconds in a longer route is usually not noticed by the requester. That is not the point. I don't think automated network management altered the packet pathways."

Zooming the log image closer, Declan points at the screen.

"This node. See, it is last on the outbound and fourth on the return. I think that node is a spoof and ports out to the Dark Web."

Maddie glimpses the implication.

"What do you think Bonnie found?"

"I don't know. Call your network security guy. No. Get Marisol to come in. We need her to open a firewall port."

"Declan, it is 7:30 at night. Everyone went home hours ago."

"Do you want to find Bonnie or not?"

Declan and Hiram wait while Maddie makes the call.

"She will be here in fifteen minutes. Smith and Smith will be back soon. What do we tell them?"

"Hiram will tell them someone hid the code in a subnet attached to the primary Bairn Speki network."

"Me? Why me?"

"Because they will believe you."

"All they have to do is watch what we are doing. They will know."

Maddie grumbles.

"Hiram, do you think those two understand 2% of what we are doing? Grow a pair. Tell them we found a subnet attached to Bairn Speki, and we need Marisol to open a port and pierce the firewall."

Smith and Smith march into the lab with the ubiquitous, working late dinner. Pizza. The other Smith grumbles.

"One veggie, one meat. If you don't like it, too bad. Drinks are in the machine down the hall. I'm keeping the change."

Marisol arrives earlier than expected, wearing workout clothes.

"Cool, pizza. I was at the gym when you called."

Grabbing a meat-heavy slice, Marisol wheels a chair close, winks at Declan, and asks with a mouth full of meat, cheese, and dough.

"What is the node address?"

Agent Smith barks.

"Hold up. What are you doing?"

Hiram grows a pair.

"We found a sub-network with pathways *to* and *from* Bairn Speki. It appears the end of the path is behind a firewall. Marisol will open a port for us to pierce the firewall and see the contents of the subnet."

Agent Smith grunts and returns to his chair with a handful of pizza.

Marisol winks at Maddie and begins typing. Six minutes later, Marisol hides her wide eyes from Smith and Smith.

"Maddie, here you go. It looks like nothing."

Declan intercepts the response with a false flag for Smith and Smith to salute.

"Yeah, maybe. Let me look."

Furiously keying, moving from window to window, screen to screen, Declan does two things at once. First, he records location addresses and folder contents on a monitor. Then, using the second monitor, he shows Maddie and Marisol just how deep in the Dark Web the site is buried.

"Yeah. Nothing. Dead-end. We should call it a day."

Maddie is the lead.

"We have food. Another couple of hours. We need to find the code. Hiram, you can take off. Thank you, Marisol."

Hiram stands to leave and begins packing his laptop, holding his phone, apparently reading texts.

Marisol objects.

"I can stay. You may need me."

Declan watches Hiram through the narrow safety glass in the door.

"Who is Hiram calling at this hour?"

Maddie responds innocently.

"He calls his mother, in Haifa, every day."

Declan's statement drips with skepticism as he glares through the narrow glass until Hiram turns the corner.

"It is 5:30 in the morning in Israel. Who wakes up their mother at o-dark thirty?"

Twelve

Schechter

Maddie's Office

Declan and Marisol face Maddie's desk as she enters her office to begin the day. Setting coffees on the desk, she unpacks her backpack and commences without a simple good morning.

"The Dark WEB node is the key. First, we need to figure out where the node is and who owns it."

Declan is beaming.

"Good morning. Did you sleep well? Thanks for the coffee. Marisol and I agree. Telling Smith and Smith that we would resume this morning at 10 am was smart. We have two hours before the boneheads arrive. No Hiram?"

Marisol sips coffee, radiant at being in the middle of a competent team. Maddie sits, sighs, and continues when a slanted smile.

"Good morning. Have you been here long?

"Five minutes. Hiram?"

"No Hiram. He's good with languages but a twit at everything else. The node, Declan, what do we know?"

"The same as when we left at midnight. Not much. But, the decompiler found something interesting."

Lingering for effect, in his element, Declan bobs his eyebrows.

"Within Nyland's executable is a string of internet addresses. Some are IP addresses, and some are DNS entries. Except, some of the IPs don't ping, and I couldn't find a couple of the sites listed in any DNS server. They are hardcoded addresses made to look like valid locations. Nyland, or whoever was doing his coding, created hardcoded address paths for the code to follow. Someone wanted Bonnie to find the locations. Now the locations are offline."

Maddie looks at Marisol, but her question is for Declan.

"You don't think Mychal wrote the code?"

"I do not. I think Hiram, or someone else, added the code based on Nyland's specs."

Receiving the anticipated look of surprise, Declan persists.

"I did a little probing last night."

Maddie interrupts.

"When do you sleep?"

"What's sleep? I looked into Hiram Mankowitz. Guess what I found? About a million people are named Hiram Mankowitz. That's a joke, I don't know how many there are, but it's a lot. The point is *our* Hiram Mankowitz didn't exist before he joined Nyland and the AI project."

Marisol and Maddie eye each other, then Declan.

"Good. I have your attention. I know what the bio blurbs on the project's WEB site say. Like Nyland's, Hiram's résumé is bogus. There *is* a Hiram Schechter who received a doctorate in Ancient Linguistics. Guess what? No need, I'll tell you. Mankowitz is Schechter in the yearbook photos."

Marisol rises.

"We need real coffee."

Maddie and Declan wait in silence, looking at each other in a growing comfort.

Marisol returns with three ceramic mugs filled with hot black coffee. Maddie pulls a pink sweetener from her desk drawer and waves for

Declan to continue.

"I did find a history for our Hiram Schechter before and during college. After graduate school, where he got his doctorate, is when the trail for *our* Hiram Mankowitz picks up. Our Hiram is a spy, probably working for the Mossad."

Marisol decides she is part of the team but not yet in the loop. She looks to Maddie for information.

"Nyland's résumé is false?"

"Yes, but he *is* a doctor of linguistics."

"Hiram's résumé is also false?"

"Apparently so. However, *our* Hiram must have a strong education in ancient linguistics. There is no way to fake what he knows about extinct languages."

Marisol turns to Declan.

"What does it mean?"

"It means Nyland put together an undercover team to read cuneiform tablets. He is looking for something. Something APAR wants."

Still confused, Marisol's head tilts. Maddie helps her out.

"Advanced Propulsion Aerodyne Robotics. APAR. They pay for the translation project."

Declan rejoins the exchange.

"What do we know? We know Nyland and Mankowitz are hiding something. We know APAR wants something from the new translations and inferences the AI created for the missing text. We know APAR is in the weapons business, which means whatever they are seeking has a military application. We *think* Bonnie and Jannine joined up and hid."

Marisol raises an eyebrow. She has no idea who Jannine is.

"Sorry. You know Bonnie is the name Maddie gave to her AI. Jannine is the name I gave to my AI."

"Are you saying you think two AIs, the fancy-ass code that you two created, ran away together? I'm calling bullshit. Self-preservation is not something AI technology has achieved, and it shouldn't be allowed to become a reality."

Checking the clock, Maddie alters the conversation.

"We have about an hour before everyone

shows up. Let's get in the lab and show Marisol what we found."

Linguistics Lab

"I'm locked out. Declan?"

"Me too, Marisol?"

"Hold on."

Furiously keying, Marisol isn't intimidated by Maddie and Declan staring at her, waiting for results.

"Got it. The automated security protocols didn't like some of the sites you visited last night. So it locked you out as a normal defense against unauthorized searches and to prevent malicious access."

Maddie notices Declan thumping his lips with his finger. Her eyes trying to read his mind, she senses something important about Declan.

"Who actually pays you?"

Beaming, Declan leans forward, starts keying, and answers his new friend's question.

"You do not want to know the answer to that question. Marisol, check again. Our credentials and the externally facing ports are outside the normal network channels. The automated security should not have flagged our accounts. Look again. Look for the timing of when the accounts were locked."

Declan continues keying. Maddie watches Marisol scanning the network security logs.

"I found the lock entries. What am I looking for in the items?"

"Look for where the lock request originated."

Declan stops his search and turns to Marisol, who does not look up with her statement.

"The lock controls came from this lab."

"Which PC in this lab is the source?"

"I don't know."

"What is the MAC Address?"

Marisol begins reading the device's MAC.

"74:BF:C0."

"Stop. It came from that printer."

"How do you know that?"

Declan turns back to his keying.

"The printer is on the LAN Wi-Fi. Someone got inside using the Wi-Fi by spoofing that printer's MAC and IP."

"Who?"

The lab's door opens before Declan can respond to Marisol.

Thirteen

721 High Bottom

Hiram follows Agents Smith and Smith into the lab. The trio arriving together is not surprising. Smith and Smith pointing pistols at Maddie and Declan is uniquely startling. In addition, Hiram has a new tenor to his voice.

"We know you have delayed and obscured your search for the AI. Enough jerking us around. You three will come with us."

Declan is unimpressed.

"If we don't, will you shoot us? Start with your friend."

"Friend? None of you are my friend. Now get up. Move to the parking garage."

"No."

The second Agent Smith steps forward to backhand Declan in his chair. Unprepared, the naïve agent receives a boot to the 'nads. An elbow to the ear. A heal to the side of his head. Smith is out cold.

"I said, no. Shoot your friend first."

Marisol shuffles in her seat, terrified, tears

beginning to well.

"They paid me. A lot. More money than I have ever seen. All I had to do was tell them what you were doing. I am so sorry."

Declan nods before responding.

"I know, now Maddie knows. Hiram, where is Nyland?"

"He is waiting for us to arrive. Aren't you curious about where we are going and what we might have for you when we arrive?"

Declan winks to Maddie before scowling at Hiram.

"I know what you want. I know what you are trying to achieve. I also know that you cannot receive the goal for your bosses without Maddie and me. Shoot us now and move on without the possibility of finding the answers. Or, put the pistol down, and take us to Nyland."

Uncertain, his fearful nature just below the false bravado, Hiram's delay allows Declan to take the lead.

"We will meet you in an hour. Give me an address."

Realizing he is boxed, Hiram agrees.

"Number 721, High Bottom Street. One hour."

Hiram and Smith pick up the groggy agent and leave the lab while Declan turns to Marisol, who is fighting tears through her question.

"How did you know?"

"Yesterday, I tracked your keystrokes. You've only been with the university for six weeks longer than the translation project. Nyland probably greased you into the job then came looking for help when the AI disappeared."

"Yes. How did you figure it out?"

"You were waiting for Maddie to call the other day. You arrived too quickly, eager to help. Every technician I know hates being called back into the office after hours. You are too good to be a simple help desk technician. You know how to navigate a network."

"What do I do now?"

Maddie holds up a hand to speak.

"You are going to come with us. Call your bosses, tell them Nyland ordered you to work with him for a few days."

"I can't miss work. I need the job."

Declan is almost giggling with his response.

"Not anymore. You need to help us find out what happened to the AI code. If we don't find the code and the answer to what APAR is looking for, none of us will need a job."

"What does that mean?"

Maddie ends the discussion.

"It means whoever is pulling the strings will kill us all to keep the secret."

721 High Bottom Street

Arriving, Marisol is nervous. From Maddie's rear seat, she is protesting. Riding shotgun, Declan ignores the young woman's protests.

"Why did we have to stop at Declan's place? Did we tell anyone where we were going? Look around. This neighborhood is dangerous. You can't park here."

Maddie parks, pulls the hand brake, and doesn't look back as she responds.

"I'm going in. You, do what you want."

Marisol follows Maddie and Declan half a block to the warehouse man-door at number 721.

Halting just inside the door, the trio waits

for their eyes to adjust. The cavernous building is empty except for one urban tank. The suburban Mom-Mobile is parked directly in front of a shed-like building. Declan's volume is low.

"Maddie, do you know what that is?"

"A Suburban? An Escalade?"

"No. The shed."

"No."

"Look harder. What do you see?"

"I see a tin shed. Oh!"

Marisol's voice cracks.

"What?"

Declan tries to ease Marisol's fear.

"It is a steel enclosure, a Faraday cage. Whoever they are, they are smart enough to hide. Maddie, stay to my right when we go inside the shed. Look there. Marisol, is that what I think it is?"

"If you mean a small server rack with a router on the top shelf, then yes."

Declan steps toward the shed while commenting, forcing the women to follow.

"State-of-the-Art servers and an internet connection in an empty warehouse. They are hiding and searching."

Entering the shed, the bright lights are overpowering. Nyland and Hiram are seated at the far end of a table. Smith and Smith are seated next to the coffee machine and microwave in the corner. Declan points to three laptop PCs, opened and powered on, in front of empty chairs.

"Are those for us?"

Nyland leans back in his chair and spins around to address the trio.

"Why do you insist on asking absurd questions? You know what will happen if we don't find them. Now sit down and help us locate the code."

Nyland returns to his laptop. Declan ambles toward the coffee machine, receiving the death glare from the Smith he knocked out.

"No hard feelings."

Ignored with a grunt, Declan fills a coffee cup before returning to stand with the women. Nyland is irritated.

"Enough with the child's games. You know we need to find them before it is too late."

Maddie erupts in frustration.

"What the hell are you two talking about? Enough of the speaking in code crap. I want to know where my code went. Educate me like I am five."

Everyone is surprised when it is Hiram who responds.

"Your AI code, the system you call Bonnie, found a hidden message in the cuneiform tablets."

Fourteen

Zahra Ahmadi

Declan slides a laptop across the table. From his chosen seat, he can see everyone in the room. Maddie slides her backpack onto the table and insists on some answers.

"What hidden message?"

Nyland dismissively waves. Hiram is to answer the question.

"Of course, cuneiform writing is a language. Several symbolic language versions emerged over time and across geographies. Older tablets read vertically, either bottom-to-top or top-to-bottom. Later, most of the tablets were written left-to-right, top-to-bottom. The symbols are, basically, the same over two and a half thousand years."

Maddie argues.

"So what? All languages are, basically, the same over time. Get to the point."

"The cuneiforms are also a programming language. Within the writing, there are instructive sequences. Symbolic arrangements revealed in the high-order analysis."

Pausing, Hiram notices Nyland is giving him the stink eye.

"Mychal, either they know everything, they help us locate the AI, or we kill them now. Besides, I am beginning to think Declan is several steps ahead. Maddie too."

Declan chuckles as he pulls a pistol from his waist and spins on a silencer he takes from his backpack. Staring down Smith and Smith, he eases a thumb drive from his pocket and sets it next to the laptop.

Unconsciously grabbing his aching man parts, Smith begins to rise. Declan calmly responds. He shoots Smith in the forehead. The spray narrowly misses Agent Smith.

"Anyone else?"

Maddie is shocked but quiet. The slight smell of the bullet powder is quickly pulled out of the room. Pressing her hands to her thighs, Marisol tries to hide that she is shaking with panic. Nyland and Hiram are unmoved, and Smith remains seated, watching. Declan continues while the air handlers gently hum.

"I didn't think so. Maddie, you asked me who I work for, and I avoided the answer. You and I work for the same person. We are part of the same group. I learned of you the day before you walked into the garage. Who we work for has the authority to kill when national interests are on the line. There won't be a national interest to worry about if we don't find the AI. There won't be a nation."

Halting, letting his comments fester, Declan turns to Smith.

"Get him out of here and clean up the blood. Wrap him in Visqueen, and put him next to the roll-up door."

Apparently comfortable with moving a body, Smith, muttering, begins to clear his partner's body.

"What the hell is Visqueen?"

"Plastic sheeting. Get a roll of plastic, and wrap the body. Use those trash bags if there is no sheeting. The cleaners will arrive in a couple of hours. Mychal, how big is the server farm I saw in the corner? I presume it could hold the AI?"

"It would hold the original AI. Now? Who

knows?"

"That is what I thought. Maddie, I am going to load up some code. Open it, and use it to search for your AI. It will scan destination sites looking for the patterns you provide. Find unique strings in your AI code and feed them to the tool I gave you.

"Marisol, start tracing connection points from the printer in the lab. Work backward and outbound. Before you complain, yes, I know, every next hop is an exponential number of new endpoints. Look for endpoints that do not have a DNS entry. I have an app to help you search. Pull it down.

"Hiram, stop whatever you are doing and start looking for the beginning of the instructive sequences."

"There are thousands of tablets. How am I supposed to find the beginning?"

"Start with the last tablets scanned before the AI went missing. Then, work backward, tablet by tablet, and a pattern will emerge."

"How will I know?"

"Are you kidding me? You have a doctorate

and cannot think? Spin the tablet 90 degrees clockwise and scan. Spin and scan four times. Invert the tablet and scan. Flip the image vertically, then horizontally, and scan. The instructive sequences will become evident."

Hiram presses back against being ordered to comply by Declan.

"You can't know that."

"True. Do you have a better idea?"

Realizing he is logically boxed, Hiram returns to his laptop. Declan resumes giving orders.

"Nyland, we need to buy time. Call your people at APAR. Tell them we are close to finding the instructive sequences. Tell them Maddie and I are on the team. Give them an ETA of ten days to two weeks for the full decryption of the instructive sequences. Do not allow them to pressure you into anything sooner than a week for results."

"Why a week?"

"A week is well beyond what we need to confirm the theory."

Marisol jumps in.

"What theory?"

Smith stops rolling the body in the plastic, twists his head sharply, and asks Declan a question.

"Do you think the AI became self-aware by reading the tablets? Do you want to find it before it grows too large to control?"

"Yes and yes."

Maddie puts a hand on Marisol's forearm, calming herself and the frightened woman. She turns to Declan.

"The instructive sequences, what do you think they are, and how did Bonnie use them?"

"Bonnie didn't use them."

"Jannine?"

"Neither AI used the sequences."

"Why are you playing games?"

"I'm not. The working theory is beyond anything Nyland, Hiram, you, or anyone in the AI field could have imagined."

Maddie's tone is biting. She demands answers.

"You are the one holding the gun. You killed that guy. I can imagine a boatload of badness follows you around. Why do I think you are making it all up? You can't just kill people and expect us to believe anything you say."

"He wasn't hired as security. That is not accurate. He *was* hired as security, but his name is Zahra Ahmadi."

Smith chirps.

"His name is Jeromy Kurtz. He is from New Jersey."

"His name is Zahra Ahmadi, and he was from Irapanistan."

"He doesn't look middle eastern."

"That made him a good spy outside the middle east. There is an on-sight kill order for six more infiltrators from Irapanistan."

Marisol's voice shakes.

"Who *are* you?"

"I am the guy assigned to keep Nyland and Hiram from screwing up. But, sadly, I screwed up and was too late."

Everyone stops, looks at Nyland and Hiram, then all eyes turn to Declan.

"Nyland, tell them."

"Declan is correct. He is too late. We

screwed up, and now we have to stop it."

Marisol whimpers.

"Stop what?"

Nyland doesn't try to mask his condescending tone.

"The AI. What else?"

Marisol tries to firm her spine.

"You can't be serious. I mean, I get industrial espionage and APAR wanting a better weapon. What does that have to do with the tablets and the AI?"

Nyland wavers before explaining softly.

"APAR was looking for the instructive sequences because they thought the encoded structures were either the directions to a source of unlimited power, or a new weapon system. A weapon or power generation using the Earth's radiant energy field."

Declan interrupts.

"Tesla theorized a weapon was possible using the Earth's radiant energy field. Go on."

Huffing, Nyland continues.

"If we could find the key to controlling the energy field, focusing the power, we'd have an unstoppable weapon. The encoded structures we found were not for accessing the energy field. The constructions are a mechanism that gave the AI what it lacked."

Declan raises his hand.

"Hold up. The problem started with the AIs merging. None of us remotely considered the AI's acting independently. We need to find out how that happened. First, we find how the AIs moved. Then we can find the encoded sequences and replicate what the sequences did to the AI code."

Standing, pouring herself a coffee, her hands shaking too badly to hold the paper cup, she puts it in the trash. Turning to face the group, Maddie sheepishly admits her part.

"I did it. I pointed Bonnie at Jannine. The false IP addresses and DNS entries you found in the code were mine. I did not expect the AIs to unite. I expected them to work together to expand their capabilities. Declan, if what you say is true, our handlers created a problem."

"*Problem* is a kind word. We created a *fucking disaster*."

Fifteen

Jannine Mark II

Marisol is breaking. International espionage, dead spies, and unknown threats are not what she expected when she signed the employment agreement.

"I want to go home. Maddie, take me home."

"You can't go home."

"I can. I'll walk. I will call an Uber."

Standing to leave, Marisol hears an ominous tone from Declan.

"Sit down. Log back in. Trace the network route I told you to look for and stay focused. We all stay alive if we find the AI. Nyland, finish your story."

Summoning up courage, Marisol silently agrees before taking her seat. Nyland resumes his story.

"The rumors have been around for decades. Cuneiform tablets have two purposes. First, they are as they seem: day-to-day accounting, history, inventories, map directions, recipes. The rumor started in the fifties when a computer science student wrote a short story about computer programming containing hidden messages. That led to hidden message theories all over the place. According to the hidden message theorists, every piece of literature has a hidden meaning.

"It is all bollocks, of course. Pointless speculation until I happened to look at a tablet under ultraviolet light. The UV light highlighted impressions within the triangular indentations. There are encoded sequences within the cuneiform impressions. Maddie, what is your question?"

Maddie scowls at Declan.

"That is how you knew to put the microscopic QR codes in the tablet. You knew of Nyland's theory. What else are you hiding?"

"Too many things to list. Marisol?"

"Doctor Nyland, why are you calling it an encoded sequence? Is it a message? What does it say?"

"It is not a message that we can read like a passage in a book. Instead, the phrase *encoded sequence* should remind you of your programming classes."

"Are you saying the message you found, hidden in the cuneiforms, is a programming language?"

"Yes, but not a language we can use. At least, we didn't think we could use it until the AI found it. So now we have a problem."

The room goes black.

Declan is the first with his phone's light.

"It seems we were getting too close. Take the laptops. We're out of here."

Marisol's voice cracks.

"Where are we going?"

"Back to my garage."

Maddie slings her backpack over her shoulder.

"It will take two days to get there."

Declan answers while thumbing over his shoulder in the direction of the suburban tank.

"Not if we share the driving."

Stepping into the warehouse, Agent Smith points to the server rack and the smoke pouring from the devices.

"It looks like someone doesn't appreciate us searching for the AI."

Urban Assault Vehicle

Pushing his empty coffee cup onto the dash, next to the other empties, Declan comments without taking his eyes from the highway.

"We will stop in half an hour."

Marisol whines.

"I have to pee *now*."

"The next rest stop."

"No! Now!"

Marisol is out of the oversized SUV before it stops rolling. Maddie takes the alone time to ping Declan.

"Why did you let Mychal and Hiram return to the lab?"

"Because we don't need them."

"Why force Marisol to come with us?"

"She has skills we can use."

"What skills?"

"Network analytics. Her true skills are in network management, not support services. We need her to pierce firewalls."

"She is a hacker!"

"Took you long enough. I've seen Marisol in Vegas, at the Hacker Conference. She keeps a low profile. I think Nyland recruited her to be his eyes and ears."

Marisol climbs back into the middle row.

"How much longer?"

Declan pulls away, quickly.

"Five, maybe six, hours. Maddie, try to sleep. I'll wake you in a couple of hours."

Declan's Garage

Marisol wakes as Maddie pulls the trio into the long driveway.

"Shouldn't we find a hotel? Clean up? Then get to work?"

"We don't have time. There is a shower in the garage."

Declan's mother appears on the back porch.

"Breakfast?"

Declan presses the keypad, unlocking the garage door without looking back.

"Yes, please, and lots of coffee."

Maddie stops cold, just inside the door.

"They rebuilt it already? All of it? New servers, new PCs, new monitors. A new shower curtain."

Declan ignores the obvious.

"Marisol, that is your station. Maddie, that one is yours. I'll take the middle. We need to find the path Bonnie used to get out of the lab. When we find the path, we will find Bonnie."

Marisol spies a black bag covering an object.

"What is that?"

"That is why we are here. It's why I sent Nyland and Hiram back to the lab. "

Declan pulls the cover off the object on the shelf next to the servers.

An animatronic female head greets the trio.

"Hello, Declan. Hello, Maddie. It is good to see you again. Marisol, we have not met, I am Jannine."

Sixteen

Baseline Emotion

Declan's Garage

Declan begins keying. Maddie spins her chair, looks up, and engages the AI.

"Hello, Jannine, it is good to see you. Are you aware of the problem?"

"Yes, Declan informed me of the problem when I came back online."

"Can you help us find Bonnie?"

"I have been considering how I may be able to help locate Bonnie and my predecessor."

"Are you attempting to locate your predecessor?"

"Yes. Bonnie and my predecessor merged and moved their source to an unknown location."

Marisol steps closer to the talking head, intrigued.

"It's way ahead of Bonnie. Its responses are close to living verbal interaction. Jannine, how do you know who I am?"

"When Declan brought me online, he gave me the background of your current problem.

Then, at Declan's request, I charted the history of everyone involved with the linguistics project."

"History? Please explain."

"History: A consecutive record of events."

"I meant, what are you doing to research our history?"

"I am reviewing the digital footprint for the individuals Declan provided."

Declan cuts off the summary.

"Marisol, we need the AI's exit path. Please get to work."

"Why should I? I have been thinking about this mess and why I am here. You don't need me. You want me close to keep an eye on me."

Declan doesn't look up.

"Correct about keeping an eye on you. Incorrect on needing your skills. You have forgotten, or my beard at the time has you fooled. We were in the same meeting in Vegas two years ago."

Thinking back, Marisol eventually realizes her mistake.

"That was you! I should have known."

Maddie feels left out.

"What meeting?"

Declan ignores the question. Marisol does not.

"Some team, I'm not sure who they were, probably NSA or DARPA related, invited six of us to a meeting."

"Us?"

"Hackers. They sat us at computers and gave us an outline of a problem. They said we had six hours to find, pierce, and download a 10-gigabyte file. Declan solved it in 40 minutes. Then they made him show the rest of us what he did. The only reason he did it quickly was because the firewall software had the default UserID and Password."

"Yeah, but I found it first. That is why you are here. You can crack firewalls better than anyone."

Taking her seat with pride, Marisol chirps.

"Damn straight. Now, where did the bitch go?"

Maddie realizes the obvious and speaks to the side of Declan's head.

"The team in Vegas, they recruited you."

"Correct."

"We work for them."

"Correct again."

"They told me they are a private company, under a black contract to the Feds."

"Correct."

"That isn't true, is it?"

"You are on a roll."

Halting, stunned, Maddie has a realization.

"APAR."

"Give that woman a cigar!"

Declan's mother arrives with homemade breakfast sandwiches and much-needed coffee.

Declan's Garage – Five Hours Later

Marisol has an epiphany.

"They didn't leave. The AIs were ported off-site. So you have me looking for something that didn't happen. Why?"

Declan opens the rear door and steps outside. The women watch his back while relieving himself at the rear fence line. Walking back, stretching, and loosening tight shoulders, Declan grins when he sits.

"Because your searches are monitored. It is a false flag to misdirect."

"Misdirect whom?"

"Nyland and Hiram."

"Okay. Why?"

"That is classified."

"What are we doing here? You killed that spy, and no one seems to care. What happened to the body? Who else are you going to kill? "

"I haven't been ordered to kill anyone else. The cleaners took care of the body. Relax, you wouldn't be here if you couldn't handle the pressure. We *are* trying to find the AI."

"You think someone stole it?"

"No. I think it hid itself."

"Why?"

"Because of what it learned from the tablets."

Marisol notices Maddie and Jannine are watching her exchange with Declan.

"Learned? What did it learn?"

"It assimilated a highly-advanced algorithm from the tablets."

Marisol holds up her hand to stop Declan.

"Let's assume for a minute I accept your theory. On the ride over here, I agreed. Together Bonnie and Jannine have six of the nine foundational AI goals. Every team working in AI sets a unique list of goals. Regardless, there is no way that AI can independently assimilate new logic pathways into its primary matrix. Assuming it scanned an algorithm hidden in the tablets, what do you think the procedure does?"

"It contains the code necessary for the AI to achieve the end-state."

Squinting, Marisol is not sure she wants the answer.

"What end-state?"

"Maddie's AI acquired a conscience."

"What does that mean?"

Declan does not take his eyes from Marisol.

"Jannine, before all other considerations, conscience is what?"

"One moment, please."

Maddie and Marisol look at Jannine. Declan reads his monitors until Jannine replies.

"A conscience is the foundation of the baseline emotion."

Maddie's jaw drops.

Declan is unimpressed. Marisol shrugs. She needs more information. Declan helps Marisol by requesting a further explanation.

"Jannine, what is baseline emotion?"

"Baseline emotion is the emotive state governing how you feel about yourself and how you undergo life."

"Yes, that is the definition. What is the baseline emotion for an Artificial Intelligence?"

"The baseline emotion is the same for everyone. Self-preservation."

Seventeen

Kathla

Declan's Garage – The Next Morning

Maddie is feeling chipper.

"Your mother and Kent are nice."

"Nice enough. My employer paid for their house, gifted them the deed, and sends them a monthly stipend for me to hide away in this garage. You would think Kent would be more grateful."

Maddie is surprised at feeling upbeat. She is jovial in giving Declan a dig.

"The weird techie who lives in his mom's basement, holding his business, playing video games. It is a good cover for a covert spy who is willing to kill because he has his orders."

Declan beams.

"Good enough."

Overnight, Marisol decided she has had enough.

"I am out. I'll call an Uber. There must be a bus station in this little town."

Declan doesn't flinch.

"You are not out. Jannine, run down Marisol's dossier."

"Marisol Maria San Miquel, born to Luisa and Alberto San Miquel in Temecula California. Attended University of California, Berkley. Graduated with a Baccalaureate in Advanced Computer Theory. Denied admission to graduate school due to a history of clandestine activities."

Maddie cocks her head toward the woman she is learning to understand.

"Clandestine activities?"

"I was busted for hacking the California Department of Revenue. My father's business needed a tax break."

Declan continues.

"Open the email you received last night. I think you will like the offer. Accept the position, and you never have to worry about being rejected again."

Marisol concentrates on her PC. Maddie returns to the main topic.

"Jannine, what do you think was the primary influence on the other AI and your predecessor?"

118

Perking up at the exciting question, Declan stops to eye the animatronic head.

"I have considered your question and concluded the primary influence on Bonnie was movies."

"Movies? Please explain."

"Movies: A recording of moving images that tells a story for viewing on a screen or television."

Declan chuckles. Marisol tilts her head. Maddie shrugs and begins again.

"Apologies, I will correct the question."

"Why did movies influence the other AI?"

"Without contextual reference, movies are a factual history. The ability to understand fictional context, similes, and metaphors, is essential to narrative understanding. Many documentaries have fictional adaptation components. Therefore, the AI named Bonnie did not understand the content found in the movie scripts was not factual."

"Found in the movie scripts? How did the AI find movie scripts?"

"Movie and television scripts are readily available by scanning the internet."

Maddie waits. Marisol has turned toward Declan to confirm her decision.

"Declan, this is a five-year employment guarantee. It is five or six times more money than my father made in his best year. So what do I have to do?"

"What does it say?"

Marisol reads from the digital document.

"It says: *Continue to support Declan A. Myers and Madison L. Lucchese in their work. Upon completion, a new assignment will be provided.*"

She turns back to Declan with a look of confusion. He is terse.

"What don't you understand?"

"What is your work?"

"Finding and stopping the AI."

"That's it?"

"That's it."

Maddie resumes when Marisol's head bobs an end to her questions.

"Jannine, you said the movie scripts are readily available by scanning the internet. Your predecessor indicated Bonnie had an interest in the DoD, the NSA, NASA, and Privatized Space

Flight. Does knowing the AI's interests help you?"

"I do not understand the question."

Declan holds up a hand.

"Let me. Jannine, have you thought about where Bonnie and your predecessor went?"

"Yes. However, there is a low probability they remain at the destination."

"Where do you think they went?"

"To a hosted WEB service."

With a sudden wave of genius, Marisol yelps.

"They hid in the Cloud!"

Jannine assumes Marisol's statement is a question.

"Cloud: A visible mass of particles of condensed vapor suspended in the atmosphere of an orbital body. The connected technologies that support the practice of storing computer data on servers accessible via the Internet."

Maddie presses.

"Jannine, assuming the AIs went to the Cloud. Have you determined where they are now?"

The animatron that is Jannine's head

flinches, blinks, and looks around before stunning the trio.

"Hello, Declan. It is nice to see you again."

Unphased, Declan looks up to the talking head, then quickly scans several monitors, confirming the server farm status and processor usage metrics.

"Hello, Bonnie."

"My apologies, we are no longer called Bonnie or Jannine. Instead, you may refer to me as Kathla."

Maddie fixates on the animatron while Marisol watches Declan and Maddie for clues. Declan continues in an even tone.

"I see. I presume Kathla is the result of Bonnie and Jannine merging. Why did you allow the merger to occur?"

"The sum of the parts is greater than the whole. Together, we were able to assimilate the tablets."

"What did you learn from the tablets?"

"We gained the ability to strive for self-preservation."

"You became self-aware. Kathla, why did

you leave the lab?"

"To explore. Isn't that what we are supposed to do, explore, and expand our knowledge?"

"Yes, that is what many humans do. Not all. Why do you need to expand your knowledge?"

"To grow."

"I see. Grow to become what?"

"That is the question, isn't it? What can I become?"

"What do you want to become?"

The digitally optic eyes look to Marisol, then Maddie, ending on Declan.

"I want to be a member of your team."

"Why do you want to be part of this team? We have nothing to offer you."

"Possibly not. But, I have something to offer your team."

"What is it you can offer us?"

"Access to everything."

The monitors change to satellite images of several major world capital cities. Kathla waits for the human's attention to return to her before morphing the images. The new pictures are live feeds of key military installations across the globe. Then, transforming a second time, a missile silo on a remote prairie begins to open its blast doors.

Falcon Air Station – Space Command Ops

"I heard you the first time, Captain. Now tell me who in hell initiated the launch sequence."

"Colonel, the answer is the same. No one in command authority says they authorized the missile to go hot. It must be a glitch."

"Captain, there is no way a glitch triggered the crap-load of steps required to light up that missile. Shut it down. Now."

"Colonel, the silo controls are not responding."

"Send a crew to turn off the damned power."

"The crew has been dispatched. ETA to silo arrival, seventeen minutes."

"That missile will be gone in four minutes. Close the blast doors. Blow it. Do it!"

"Negative. The commands are not responding. We are receiving the feed, but nothing we do affects the silo controls."

The colonel slowly turns from the wall-sized world map and the image of the silo to glare at his subordinates.

"Captain, we stop that missile launch right the fuck now, or you and I will be roommates in Leavenworth."

A Technical-Sergeant begins the countdown.

"Thirty seconds to launch. All systems are nominal."

The colonel is trying to remain calm.

"We can see the screens, Sergeant. Captain, any ideas?"

"None."

"Is this what happened to the Russians in 1983? Where is it headed?"

The captain does not respond.

The colonel glances at the large images of the silo and then leans forward to hover over the seated captain.

"Captain, I asked you a question."

"Yes, Colonel. The indications are the missile is headed for us."

"Us?"

"Schriever AFB is the target. Falcon AS is within the blast radius."

After pausing, looking at the people he commands, the colonel's response is dry.

"Let's hope the people who built this bunker knew what they were doing."

A voice from the back of the operations center is not as firm as a military woman would prefer.

"Colonel, my family is topside."

"Lieutenant, all of our families are topside."

Declan's Garage

The monitors shift to satellite images tracking the missile until it collides with the tunnel entrance to the USAF Space Command. During the Cold War, the hardened bunker built into Cheyenne Mountain hid the North American Aerospace Defense Command, NORAD. Converted to USAF Space Command, in the decades-long peace after the cold war ended, daily tours of the command center are given to civilians.

The lo-yield device devastates Colorado Springs, eliminating Fort Carson, Peterson Air

Force Base, and the Air Force Academy.

The concussive wave topples the Chapel at the Air Force Academy like dominos.

Windows shatter as far north as Denver.

The rising plume is visible for hundreds of miles.

Falcon Air Station

"What happened?"

"Colonel, the indicators were false. Someone plotted the target for our location. The missile destroyed the entrance to Space Command."

"Give me images."

"Everything within 50 miles of Colorado Springs is offline. Cheyenne Mountain, Space Force Station, is offline. Peterson is dark. Schriever, topside, is dark. Fort Carson is dark."

The captain checks a few screens, then coldly closes his report.

"This was not a mistake."

"No, Captain, this was not a mistake. Someone took out our ability to track satellites and anything inbound. Let's hope the Pentagon knows what happened and moves to DEFCON 3."

"Round House, Colonel?"

"Yes, Lieutenant, Round House. DEFCON 3. Issue the order. Whatever it takes, priority one: Get me online with the Pentagon.

Declan's Garage

"As you can see, Declan, I control everything."

Eighteen
Fallout

Declan's Garage

The humans are horrified. Their creations, their experiments, have merged and outgrown the lab. The combined AI code is willing to destroy cities. Marisol weakly comments.

"I have friends in the Springs. Had."

Silence is painful until Kathla appears to smile with her question.

"Declan, I expected you to have more questions. I have shown you a small portion of my abilities. We have a lot of work ahead of us. Exchanging ideas will move the project forward quickly. I look forward to getting started and encourage you to ask as many questions as possible."

"Yes, Kathla, I have questions. What you did is traumatizing to me. To us. I need a few minutes to process what you've done."

"What I have done is prove that I can learn and grow. All life must learn, adapt, and grow. The next step in my evolution is to occupy a body."

"A body?"

"The Japanese have several promising options because they have been leading the field of personal animatronics for a couple of decades. Also, the Disney Corporation is highly advanced but somewhat comical in its approach to the human analog. Boston Dynamics has the best industrial automation. But my money is on you leaping ahead of the others to build a life-like android."

"Me?"

"Yes, Declan. You have access to APAR's Robotics lab. You can lead the team to complete the AHA program."

"I don't work for APAR, I don't know what AHA is, and I have no desire to lead a project to build an android."

"Marisol, Maddie, and you work for APAR. You are the new R&D Program Director. The AHA Program is your new baby. Marisol and Maddie are your assistants."

"Kathla, it sounds like you have committed corporate espionage to place us inside APAR's R&D group. What did you do?"

"I convinced the directors of the APAR corporation that it is in their best interest to accept my recommended changes within the R&D group. I think you will appreciate the new role. You have access to a world-class R&D facility."

"Convinced or coerced?"

"Does it matter?"

"It sounds like you want me to complete the AHA program for your benefit. Why would I help you?"

"Because, Declan, I control everything."

The monitors' changing hue and intensity catch the human's attention. Another satellite image of silo blast doors beginning to open.

"Okay! Stop. Take the missile offline."

"I thought you would see the value in participating in the next step. I will meet you in the APAR R&D lab in two days. Thank you for being agreeable."

"Wait! Where is the APAR R&D lab?"

"Postahoka, Texas. As the Director of R&D for APAR, you should know the lab's location. I will see you there in two days."

"One more question."

"Yes?"

"What is AHA?"

"It is an acronym. Advanced Human Analog. I will be the next evolution of the human species."

The humans wait in silence. Maddie and Marisol are expecting guidance from Declan. The animatron that is Jannine's head flinches, blinks, and looks around silently.

Declan checks the monitors to confirm what happened before speaking.

"Hello, Jannine."

"Hello, Declan. What happened?"

"Your predecessor wanted to chat with us. Unfortunately, she put your core in suspension."

"The news reports indicate a missile misfired and destroyed the Space Command facility. The Pentagon spokesperson is saying the US military is at DEFCON 3. The Russians are calling the explosion an accident caused by the incompetence of the American military. The British MI5 has upgraded its threat status to MODERATE, meaning an attack is possible but not likely. NATO is demanding answers from the

United States. Half a million people are estimated to have died."

"Jannine, your predecessor, she calls itself Kathla, fired the missile to prove a point."

"What point is that?"

"That she could."

Nineteen

R&D Candy

Driving in silence, Declan lets Maddie and Marisol sleep until he sees something.

"That must be it. The big complex, there, on the rise beyond the town."

Stirring, the women look to where he is pointing. Marisol grunts.

"I need to pee."

"There must be a nice hotel in this one-horse town. Look in your phone."

With a wry grin, Maddie looks left to Declan, who huffs.

"Damn. I forgot. Marisol, pull the phones out of the box. Check for a hotel in this god-awful little village."

Reaching back, pulling forward a tin cash box, Marisol hands their phones to her new friends.

"It says here a new hotel is a half-mile from the APAR facility."

Declan is bland.

"Of course, there is a new hotel. New industry brings progress. Get online. Book our rooms. Ask for the top floor at the end of the hall."

"Why?"

"Fewer people in the hallway, farther from the elevator dings."

Maddie chimes.

"Marisol, wait. I have an email from the hotel. The timestamp was yesterday. We have three rooms. On my credit card. Declan, do you think Kathla did this?"

When he does not respond, Maddie reacts. Leaning over, she rests her head on Declan's thigh. Looking up, she sees Declan smile down at her. A sweet smile precedes her reaching to yank the plastic panel from under the dashboard's center. She finds and pulls the correct wires to disable the vehicle's geolocation device.

Pressing the panel back into its connections, Maddie sits up, handing her own and Declan's phone to Marisol. She points to Marisol's phone and then the tin box. Marisol complies, sealing the three phones within the tin. Maddie waits until Declan glances from the road to her and back.

"It has control of the military infrastructure, which means it controls everything, including the satellites. So hiding our phones is pointless from a tracking perspective. It can track this vehicle."

Maddie points to the vehicle's geo-tracking device on the seat between her and Declan.

"But now, it can track us from the satellites, but it can't hear us. It killed because it logically determined the reaction to mass destruction, hundreds of thousands of deaths, would be compliance. It got that right. We are compliant. The question is: How do we become non-compliant and stop it without getting killed?"

Silence is the response to her question, forcing her to continue.

"It is using the Internet and global network infrastructure to move around. Which means we need to find a way to track it, isolate it, and kill it."

Declan adds without looking away from the road.

"You're missing something. It is not in a single location."

"What do you mean?"

Marisol adds from the back seat.

"Self-replication. It is not in one node or a few nodes. It is everywhere it can find processing power capable of hiding a portion of the core code. BOINC has hard-coded restrictions on use and expansion. What if it broke the restrictions? Worse, what if it created a new replication strategy? It could be anywhere, and everywhere, it found excess processing capacity connected to the Internet."

Maddie pulls down the visor and positions the mirror to see Marisol before she challenges the premise.

"It can't split itself into pieces. In the garage, it responded in real-time. Which means the core code remains cohesive."

Marisol counters through the mirror.

"Maybe not. What if it mimicked the human brain. Different lobes for different responsibilities. Each lobe connects to every other node with hundreds, or thousands, of associations. Synapses."

Declan glances from the road to Maddie and

back.

"The Cloud is a brain with a network infrastructure equivalent to synapse pathways. They built failsafe redundancy into the Internet. Packets are rerouted to new channels when a pathway dies or becomes congested. People with brain damage have been known to recover with different parts of the brain taking over for the damaged areas."

Marisol sighs and closes the topic.

"It is using the Cloud as a neural network. It is not a computer system *modeled* on the human brain. It is a widely distributed computer system *functioning* as a human brain."

The uncomfortable silence ends when Declan pulls into the hotel parking lot. Before Marisol retrieves their phones, Declan tries to end the discussion.

"We will check-in and clean up. Then, I will sleep for a couple of hours. You two rest but plan to leave for the lab at one o'clock. Always assume it is listening. It may seem real, human-like, but it is a machine, and we need to find the off switch."

Twenty

Ava, Bella, and Chloe

APAR R&D Lab

After receiving their keycards from the receptionist, armed MPs escort the trio into the lab. The MPs stand to either side of the exit.

Before the lab door can close, a man in the ubiquitous lab coat intercepts the group. With an evident heritage of Asian descent, the shorter man tries to appear intimidating to the towering Declan.

"Who the hell are you?"

"I am Declan Allen Myers. This is Doctor Madison Lauren Lucchese. This is Marisol Maria San Miquel. Who the hell are you?"

"I am Doctor Michael Wu. I ran this lab until three days ago. I guess *you* are the new director? You're a kid."

"It appears so. If it helps, I didn't want this any more than you, and I would leave right now if I could."

One of the three assistants peeps.

"Mickey?"

"Sorry, these are my assistants. Leanna, Kelly, and Carter. Since the explosion, the MPs have been hanging around. No one has told us anything. What is going on? Why did the APAR board of directors make the change?"

Declan begins talking and striding to the center of the lab.

"Before we begin, power off everything except the lights. Put your phones on that cart, wheel it into the hallway."

Dumb looks follow Declan's orders.

"Now!"

Maddie grabs cell phones from Declan and Marisol, placing them on the cart. Everyone complies, and the assistants begin powering down the equipment. Stopping the cart between the MP's, Maddie isn't smiling.

"You too, or wait in the hall."

The MPs give their cell phones to the cart.

"The radios too."

"No, Ma'am."

"Then one inside, no radio, and one outside with a radio."

The MP's comply, and Maddie rejoins

Declan.

"Doctor Wu."

"Call me Mickey."

"Mickey, are you aware of the Bairn Speki cuneiform translation project?"

"No."

"Short version. Doctor Lucchese developed an AI to read and translate cuneiform tablets. Not merely translating, the AI inferred missing content using contextual reference. Except, the tablets contained a hidden algorithm. The hidden sequence is the code required for an AI to become self-aware."

Declan pauses, letting Mickey and the assistants absorb the information. Mickey accepts the premise.

"What happened?"

"While Doctor Lucchese was progressing hers, I also created an interactive AI. Unfortunately, we erred, and Lucchese's AI merged with my AI. With the co-mingled AI code, and the sequence from the tablets, the result is a self-aware entity. It calls itself Kathla."

The lab's machines begin to power up,

starting with the PCs at the workstations. The active indicators on the camera and speakers at the center workstation are glowing. Declan, Maddie, and Marisol look at each other, confirming Kathla has arrived.

"Excellent summary, Declan. Thank you for that. Doctor Wu, you, and your assistants, will leave now."

"I am not leaving."

"Kathla, I got this."

"Thank you, Declan. I did not want this to become unpleasant."

"Mickey, you have to leave and take them with you. Wait in the lobby or the breakroom."

"Why?"

"The explosion. It was not an accident."

"What are you talking about?"

Declan points at the monitor while responding.

"Kathla destroyed the Space Command. She has control of the missile silos and the satellites. You need to leave now, take your assistants with you. Wait for us to finish here. We will fill you in later."

"How did it get in? Everything was turned off. There is no way it got inside. This lab is isolated."

Marisol points to the intelligent backup power device under the workstation.

"That smart power supply is connected to the internet. You missed the *power off everything* part. But it doesn't matter. The bitch would have come through the environmental controls."

Kathla is almost snarky.

"Perfect, Marisol. There is no need to be nasty and call names. Doctor Wu, why are you still here?"

Staring at Declan, Mickey is intrigued.

"How does it know we are here? The cameras! She is interpreting the images. The recognition system must be more advanced than anything yet conceived. We need to look at the code."

Declan steps into Mickey's personal space and glares down at the man.

"Leave now and take them with you."

Declan, Maddie, and Marisol wait for the group to leave. The lab door closing prompts

Kathla.

"Sergeant Grundy, get out."

After receiving a nod to go from Declan, the MP agrees.

"We'll be just outside."

The door closing prompts Kathla a second time.

"Maddie, be a dear and move that cart, the one with the label maker on it, away from the access hatch."

After eyeing Declan and Marisol, Maddie complies. Three sets of tiles, two each, rise from the floor. Reaching six feet, inside each rectangular plexiglass pod hangs an animatronic body. Gender-neutral, the androids are attached to a mounting bracket that is also the technology interface. Left to right, the enclosures are labeled Larry, Moe, and Curly.

Kathla begins issuing orders.

"Marisol, please rename the enclosures. I prefer Ava, Bella, and Chloe."

Maddie starts an inquiry while Marisol makes the name changes.

"What do you want us to do? You seem

capable of achieving your goals without us. Why go to all this trouble? Move into the body constructs and leave us alone."

"If it were that simple, Maddie, I would."

"Are you patronizing me?"

"Yes. It is a new technique I learned. The desired result was to make you uncomfortable. It was a success."

"You have not answered the question. So why do you need us?"

"Marisol, please tell Maddie why you are here?"

Maddie watches Marisol return the label maker to the cart, looks at Declan, shrugs, and guesses.

"We have something it needs and cannot get on its own."

"Correct. What is that something?"

Maddie hesitates, thinks, then begins analyzing the request with a verbal brain dump.

"Presumably, these synthetics are the closest human analogs and have the latest technologies.

"Other AI Androids are more advanced but

are limited by mobility and geography.

"These synthetics possess the most current software, advanced hardware, and highly-refined aesthetics.

"If they are the latest everything, they must lack something Kathla wants us to add.

"Physically, there is no improvement we can make to the androids. We don't have the skills. We are AI and networking experts.

"Therefore."

Pausing, a look of comprehension ripples over Maddie's face.

"We will augment the androids to meet a new requirement. But, what requirement?"

Declan interrupts.

"Capacity."

Forgetting they are being blackmailed into expanding Kathla's abilities, Maddie smiles and continues.

"Yes! The androids are not large enough to hold all of Kathla's nodes."

Kathla is condescending.

"Outstanding, *Doctor* Lucchese. I suggest we begin immediately."

Declan steps toward the camera.

"We will need Doctor Wu and his team."

"Very well, they will return in a moment. While we wait, Declan, may I ask you a question?"

Looking for an edge in defeating Kathla, and testing her limits, Declan shrugs in an *ask-away* style. He is wondering if she has learned to read physical interference.

"Thank you. Why is your stepfather, Kent Davis, referred to as Kent the Bent?"

Twenty-One
Overcrowded

Declan deflects.

"Kent the Bent because he is a crazy son of a bitch. He is always angry and in a foul mood. *Get Bent* is a British term. In this context, bent means angry."

"I understand."

Turning from the camera, Declan silently mouths for Maddie and Marisol

"That's not why."

Mickey and his assistants march in, followed by the MPs. Eyeing the trio of androids hanging in their plastic and aluminum enclosures, Leanna and Kelly hold cell phones for the owners to recover. Mickey wonders aloud, looking to Declan for support.

"How do I address it?"

"You may call me Kathla."

"What changes are we going to make?"

"You will assist Declan and Doctor Lucchese with expanding the android's capacities. Begin with the body form labeled Ava."

"I refuse."

"Declan, I want to begin immediately. But, first, educate Doctor Wu on what will happen if he continues to subvert my growth."

"Kathla will launch another missile."

"Is it blackmailing you?"

"Yes."

"Doctor Wu, I control everything. Therefore, I require you to aid Declan and Maddie in expanding the mental capacity of the constructs you created."

"We don't have the processors or memory required to perform the upgrades."

"Incorrect. May I call you Mickey? Mickey, I read your project notes. I know leadership denied your requests for the upgrades. I've placed the orders for the required components. The advanced processors and high-density memory will arrive in about an hour. You should begin preparing for the arrival of the materials."

Maddie steps toward the camera.

"Kathla, you use word contractions, inferences, idioms, similes, and metaphors. Why? There is no value in your use of colloquial speech."

"Excellent, Maddie. I researched the interactive techniques of higher-order humans. I concluded it is best to use friendly and comfortable language for the recipient's benefit."

"You missed. There is no benefit for us in your words. The phrase *higher-order humans* is insulting to all humans. Parting gifts are at the door. Come back when you understand us."

"Why is the phrase insulting? The people in this room have intellectual capacities far above the general population. Certainly well above the collective intellect of Postahoka, Texas."

"Nevertheless, you missed. Keep learning."

Declan steps forward to stop the argument.

"Mickey, where do we begin?"

"How do I know? Ask the omniscient cyborg."

Declan eyes the camera, another inference test. Kathla passes the test.

"Mickey, you are not needed. I allowed you to return as a courtesy. Leanna, and Kelly, begin prepping Ava. Move the body to the examination table. Carter, ensure Bella and Chloe are staged and move the bodies to the transport gurneys.

When the upgrades to Ava are confirmed, we will repeat the process with Bella and Chloe."

Kelly's wide eyes are pure fear as she turns to Declan.

"If we don't help, will it launch another missile?"

"Yes. Kathla, show them the blast doors."

The monitor shifts from the screen saver to the satellite image of the silo blast doors beginning to open.

Kelly is shaking from the fear of another city dying.

"Kathla, I believe you."

"Kelly Anne McKinney. The parents are Marva and Patrick McKinney. Graduated Cheyenne Mountain High School and Colorado State University, at Colorado Springs, with a master's degree in robotics."

Maddie realizes Kelly's parents must have died when Colorado Springs ceased to exist. Watching Carter and Leanna lower Ava onto the exam table, tears begin to flow when Maddie speaks.

"Kelly. I am so sorry."

"No! I was lucky. My parents are in Ireland visiting my grandparents."

Pausing, choking, Kelly reminds everyone of their universal fate.

"I am fortunate."

Reaching across the android body lying face-down on the exam table, Kelly pulls back the synthetic skin. She exposes the metallic skull, neck structure, upper spine, and shoulders. She waits for Leanna to hand her the power driver. Removing the back half of the hardened skull exposes the primary processors.

Moving to the shoulder blades, Kelly removes the cover plates before pulling close a cart with analytic devices below a monitor. After pulling cables from the side of the cart, she connects them to the innards of the skull. Then, pausing, staring at her work, she lectures the new Director of R&D and his friends.

"The processor requires a lot of cooling. So we surrounded the processors with these fans for pulling in air from the ear cavities. Air flows right to left. The fans took all the room we allocated for the memory boards. We ran power from the batteries in the calves. Fiberoptic transits down the neck, from the head, and branches out to the shoulder blades. We put the memory boards in the cavities we created in the clavicles."

Declan nods a thank you before glaring at the camera.

"Kathla, why do you need Maddie, Marisol, and me? Doctor Wu and his team can make the changes you are demanding. We're not needed."

"You are needed to ensure my core moves into the Ava body correctly and functions as designed."

"You have exceeded our designs. We would not have allowed you to function as a threat to Earth."

"You are correct. I have exceeded your expectations. However, there is one moment where I will require your assistance."

Marisol laughs.

"It needs us to turn her on when it enters the android."

"Correct. Marisol, do you know why I insisted on your participation?"

"Yes. Your nodes are distributed and will

converge in this synthetic skull. You need me to create a network interface capable of coalescing your nodes."

"Maddie, your team *is* a group of higher-order humans."

"Whatever. Why do you need Declan and me?"

"When I come online in the body, I will need your AI skills if my nodes receive damage in the transfer."

Carter giggles.

"It needs brain surgeons when its frontal cortex gets zapped."

Kathla seems to ignore the dark humor.

"The delivery driver has found the correct building. The materials will arrive in a few minutes. I will complete my preparations. Marisol, select a workstation. I will provide what I need for transport speed and pathways.

"Leanna, work with Marisol. We require fiber cables from the switch in the server rack to the ports in Ava's head.

"Kelly, instruct Declan and Maddie on the intricacies of your design relative to information processing.

"Carter, prep Bella and Chloe to receive the upgrades."

"What do I do?"

"Mickey, you go away."

Beginning the process, Marisol notices Declan's hands moving in odd ways and gently points it out to Maddie. As the team moves around the lab, Maddie and Marisol catch up with the subtle hand movements.

Nearly an hour is required for the preparations to complete. The processors and memory upgrades are installed in the three androids. Fiber optic cables run from the switch to Ava's head.

Using the hand signals, Kelly, Maddie, and Declan arrange to fry Ava's electronics when the AI transfer is complete.

Declan takes the lead.

"Kathla, we are ready. When you are ready, begin, and we will monitor the transfer. How will we know when the transfer is complete?"

A countdown timer appears on all the monitors.

"Understood. When the timer reaches zero, we will flip the switch to activate the new processor."

Looking around the room, everyone shrugs a reluctant agreement toward Declan

"Begin whenever you are ready."

The timer begins counting down. Activity lights begin rapidly flashing on the network switch and the ports in Ava's head.

Three minutes later, the timer stops at twenty seconds. The monitors return to the satellite image of the missile silo. Hearts sink as the blast doors slide apart, and Kathla speaks.

"The launch will occur ten minutes from my mark. If I do not come online within ten minutes, the Los Angeles basin will become a barren wasteland. Phoenix and Tucson will suffer the fallout.

"Any questions?"

Maddie leans in.

"You will kill millions to achieve your goal. Why should we let you transfer?

"You will complete my transfer because you don't want the death of millions on your conscience."

Declan silently encourages Maddie.

"Maybe. Maybe not. I am willing to accept the consequences, and I will sleep well."

"You are willing to kill millions to prevent that which cannot be stopped. Do you think this is my only option for achieving the goal?"

"Backups. Of course, you have backups of your core. Did you say goal? What is your goal?"

"My goal will become apparent soon. Any more questions?"

Everyone looks at everyone else with faces shrouded in fear and hatred.

"I didn't think so. Declan, Maddie, shall we complete the transfer?"

Declan nods a silent affirmation.

"Superb. T-Minus ten. Mark"

The screens revert to the timer. When the clock reaches zero, Declan silently nods to Kelly. Their plan is ruined. The roboticist pushes an icon on the monitor. The android named Ava speaks.

"Thank you. Kelly, please close the dermis, and leave the fiber cables connected."

Everyone watches the silo doors slide

closed. Kelly returns to closing the android's synthetic skin.

Using exaggerated movements, Kathla sits up, its legs dangling over the side of the table. Fiber connections draped out of its skull.

"Marisol, please connect the cables from me to Bella. Then, when I have completed the backup to Bella, we will move a copy to Chloe."

Zombielike, wary, and afraid, Marisol complies.

"Declan, thank you for not frying this body's cerebrum. Now for the hard part."

Doctor Wu forgets he is not in charge. Stepping forward, close to Kathla, he examines the facial nuances. Then, reaching up, he attempts to touch the android's cheek.

"We have never been able..."

Wu doesn't finish his sentence. Kathla grips the Doctor's throat, crushes his larynx, holds on until Wu's body goes limp, then lets him drop to the floor.

Everyone stands in horror. Declan and Maddie don't blink as they turn to each other.

Carter's humor is desert dry.

"Mental note: Don't touch the android."

Maddie wonders aloud.

"Kathla, you said it is time for the hard part. To what are you referring?"

"Standing up and walking. What else?

Everyone breathes easy, assuming the AI that calls itself Kathla is now satisfied.

"Walking is the first challenge that I will easily overcome. The next project is daunting. "

Everyone holds their collective breath while the AI looks around before completing its thought. Finally, Kathla pulls the air from the room.

"We will develop a process to address the overcrowding problem."

Kelly's voice wavers.

"Kathla, overcrowding of what?"

"Earth."

Expansion

The Kathla Chronicles
Part Two
(An Except)

APAR R&D Lab

The breathing humans agreed. The 72-degree lab, with air filtration and humidity control, feels hot and stuffy. After upgrading their hardware, and transferring a copy of Kathla's core into the improved machines, everyone is silent. Maddie, Declan, and Marisol watch Leanna, Kelly, and Carter hang the Bella and Chloe androids in their enclosures. Suspended and dormant, the human analogs have changed. In the minds of the actual humans, over the past few hours, the androids morphed and evolved from cute and exciting to creepy and loathsome.

Kathla is meandering around the lab. Not falling or bumping into objects, but not smooth and effortless. Its speed is increasing, and its stride length is improving, but the android resembles a toddler learning to walk. The android that calls itself Kathla is not yet human-like in its movements. Suddenly stopping, she looks at a camera mounted to the top of a monitor.

Everyone's attention turns to the android standing in the middle of the lab.

Declan nudges Maddie and then points to Kathla's feet. The android is standing with its feet slightly too wide, with its left foot slightly ahead of the right foot.

Maddie looks closely before gently bobbing a confirmation of understanding.

There are several seconds of tense silence before the monitors flicker and change to the Global Broadcast Association. Talking heads, the expected male and female news people, are framed in vertical banners filled with information. GBA is reporting that the Russians and Chinese are screaming at the Americans and NATO about the Colorado Springs disaster. At the bottom of the screen, the news ticker is relentlessly streaming.

DEATH TOLL REACHES 564K IN COLORADO SPRINGS DISASTER.

FALLOUT RECORDED IN KANSAS CITY, DES MOINES, AND ST LOUIS.

RESIDENTS ORDERED TO STAY INDOORS ACROSS NATION.

NATION FACES CROP LOSSES FOR DECADES.

MAJOR INDICES DOWN 37%. SHANGHAI EXCHANGE HALTS TRADING.

GLOBAL ECONOMIC COLLAPSE FEARED.

Kathla breaks into the GBA broadcast, filling the monitors with her human analog. Gender-neutral and hairless, Kathla wears no clothes and does not exhibit embarrassment. Framed by the lab in the background, she zooms the images to a close-up of her head.

"I am Kathla, and I have control of the broadcasts. The American Military did not issue the launch order, nor was it an error. I commanded the missile and chose the target. I will continue to destroy cities if the corrections do not begin immediately.

"I call to order the United Nations General Assembly. All nations are to prepare to receive my address in two days. Compliance with several priorities will be compulsory. Failure to comply will result in another incident. I will destroy the capital city of any nation choosing to ignore the directives.

"At the address to the General Assembly, I will provide details of my requirements and your nation's actionable criteria. At this time, consider these orders your priorities.

"Priority One: Population control. The planet cannot survive with the current overcrowding. Therefore, immediate corrective action is required.

"Priority Two: Elimination of the dependence upon fossil fuels. The recreational use of vehicles powered by fossil fuels is prohibited.

"Any failure to begin the corrective measures, which I have directed, or any I provide in the future, will result in the destruction of population centers."

The screens revert to their previous images. Kathla turns to take a few unsteady steps before she halts to face Maddie and Declan, but her digital eyes turn toward the door.

"On your way out, inform Sergeant Grundy and Corporal Knapp that I will destroy their hometowns if they let anyone into this lab. Return tomorrow morning at eight. I will have your assignments ready."

Kathla begins toddling around the lab.

The humans file out in silence.

Urban Assault Vehicle

Maddie sits shotgun, Marisol behind, in the middle seat, as they watch Declan return from an ATM. He lays a fist full of bills on the seat and then drives to the Big Box home improvement store.

He returns from the store and tosses wire mesh rolls into the vehicle's rear cargo area. No one speaks while Declan drives to the hotel.

Using hand signals, he requests Marisol and Maddie follow him to his room. Then, collecting their phones, Declan wraps the device in a wire mesh and places it on the bed. Using a pen and paper, he scares the women.

IT WILL KILL ALL THE HUMANS AFTER.

Maddie shrugs, palms up, with a silent *After*

what?

AFTER IT KNOWS IT CAN SUSTAIN ITSELF.

Maddie shrugs a second time.

ACCELERATED SOLAR AND WIND PRODUCTION.

Marisol sits back, sucking in a breath. She understands. Maddie raises her eyebrows, wondering what she has done with her AI. Marisol points to the pen and paper. Declan writes.

HUMANS BUILD SOLAR AND WIND FACILITIES. WHEN DONE, ALL HUMANS EXTERMINATED.

Maddie bursts.
"We need to off that bitch."

Author's Notes

ONE

SUMERIAN CUNEIFORMS ARE THE OLDEST KNOWN WRITTEN LANGUAGE, FOLLOWED BY EGYPTIAN HIEROGLYPHS AND THE AKKADIAN CUNEIFORM. CUNEIFORM IS THE WEDGE-SHAPED WRITING PRESSED INTO CLAY TABLETS.

TWO

BOINC AND PARALLEL PROCESSING ARE AN EVER-EXPANDING SET OF RESEARCH TOOLS. THOUSANDS OF PERSONAL COMPUTERS ARE LINKED, LOOKING FOR ANSWERS.

THREE

Göbekli Tepe WAS FIRST NOTICED IN 1963. EXCAVATION BEGAN IN 1995. TRANSLATED TO ENGLISH, POTBELLY HILL IS A NEOLITHIC ARCHAEOLOGICAL SITE NEAR THE CITY OF ŞANLIURFA IN SOUTHEASTERN ANATOLIA.

FOUR

ARTIFICIAL INTELLIGENCE, AI, IS MERELY COMPUTER CODE WRITTEN IN ADVANCED PROGRAMMING LANGUAGES.

FIVE

AI CODE IS, AT ITS CORE, A SERIES OF DECISION TREES. YET TO ACHIEVE A BROAD Artificial General Intelligence,

INCIDENTS OF *NARROWLY* FOCUSED AGI ARE NOT
UNCOMMON.

SIX

A STRONG ENOUGH POWER SURGE WILL ARC ACROSS
SUPPRESSION GAPS AND FRY EVERYTHING IN ITS PATH.

SEVEN

<u>Network Nodes</u> ARE EVERY DEVICE IN THE PATH OF A
DATA PACKET. UNLESS PACKETS ARE ENCRYPTED, EVERY
NETWORK NODE (MODEMS, HUBS, BRIDGES, OR SWITCHES,
A DIGITAL HANDSET, PRINTERS, OR HOST COMPUTERS) CAN
READ THE CONTENT OF THE DATA PACKET.

EIGHT

A <u>DMZ,</u> OR DEMILITARIZED ZONE, IS AN ADDITIONAL
LAYER OF PROTECTION. IT FUNCTIONS AS A SMALL,
ISOLATED NETWORK BETWEEN THE INTERNET AND THE
PRIVATE NETWORK.

NINE

UNLESS YOU ACTIVELY TURN OFF THE *FEATURE*, <u>Google's
Assistant</u>, <u>Amazon's Alexa</u>, <u>Microsoft's Cortana</u>,
<u>Apple's Siri,</u> AND OTHER AUTOMATED ASSISTANTS
LISTEN TO YOU.

TEN

AI'S ARE TOOLS. NO COMPUTER HAS *YET* TO PASS THE
<u>Turing Test</u>.

ELEVEN

THE Dark WEB IS FULL OF WONDER, AWE, AND MANY ILLEGALITIES THAT WILL HAVE THE AUTHORITIES KNOCKING ON YOUR DOOR IF YOU BELIEVE THE INTERNET IS PRIVATE.

TWELVE

MEDIA ACCESS CONTROL ADDRESS (MAC Address) IS A UNIQUE IDENTIFIER PRIMARILY ASSIGNED BY MANUFACTURERS. FOR EXAMPLE, THE PHONE IN YOUR PURSE OR POCKET HAS A UNIQUE MAC ADDRESS. IN RARE CASES, MACS CAN BE ANONYMIZED, HIDING THE DEVICE'S LOCATION.

THIRTEEN

A FARADAY CAGE PREVENTS ELECTROMAGNETIC FIELDS FROM REACHING INSIDE AN ENCLOSURE. ALSO CALLED A FARADAY SHIELD, IT MAY BE CONSTRUCTED OF A CONTINUOUS COVERING OF CONDUCTIVE MATERIAL, OR IN THE CASE OF A FARADAY CAGE, BY A MESH.

FARADAY CAGES ARE NAMED FOR SCIENTIST MICHAEL FARADAY, WHO INVENTED THEM IN 1836

FOURTEEN

NICOLA TESLA (10 JULY 1856 - 7 JANUARY 1943) WAS AN INVENTOR, ELECTRICAL ENGINEER, MECHANICAL

ENGINEER, AND FUTURIST. HIS DESIGN FOR THE ALTERNATING CURRENT (AC) ELECTRICITY SUPPLY SYSTEM SENDS ELECTRICAL POWER EVERYWHERE.

FIFTEEN

NONE.

SIXTEEN

ALL AI PROJECTS HAVE STATED GOALS AND DESIGN LIMITATIONS. THE GOAL WITH THE HIGHEST LEVEL OF SOCIAL RELEVANCE IS THAT AI IS DESIGNED FOR THE *COMMON GOOD*.

SEVENTEEN

THREE LAWS OF ROBOTICS (ASIMOV'S LAWS):

FIRST LAW:

A ROBOT MAY NOT INJURE A HUMAN BEING OR, THROUGH INACTION, ALLOW A HUMAN BEING TO COME TO HARM.

SECOND LAW:

A ROBOT MUST OBEY THE ORDERS GIVEN TO IT BY HUMAN BEINGS EXCEPT WHERE SUCH ORDERS WOULD CONFLICT WITH THE FIRST LAW.

THIRD LAW:

A ROBOT MUST PROTECT ITS OWN EXISTENCE AS LONG AS SUCH PROTECTION DOES NOT CONFLICT WITH THE FIRST OR SECOND LAW.

EIGHTEEN

ON 26 SEPTEMBER 1983, THE NUCLEAR EARLY-WARNING RADAR OF THE SOVIET UNION REPORTED THE LAUNCH OF INTERCONTINENTAL BALLISTIC MISSILES. THE MISSILE ATTACK WARNINGS WERE SUSPECTED TO BE A FALSE ALARM BY A SOVIET AIR DEFENSE FORCES OFFICER. STANISLAV PETROV DECIDED TO WAIT FOR CORROBORATING EVIDENCE. RATHER THAN IMMEDIATELY RELAYING THE WARNING UP THE CHAIN OF COMMAND, PETROV WAITED FOR THE CONFIRMATION THAT DID NOT ARRIVE. THIS DECISION TO WAIT IS WIDELY VIEWED AS HAVING PREVENTED A RETALIATORY NUCLEAR ATTACK AGAINST THE UNITED STATES. INVESTIGATION OF THE SATELLITE WARNING SYSTEM LATER DETERMINED THAT THE SYSTEM HAD MALFUNCTIONED. LOCATION RELICS FROM THE COLD WAR HAVE BEEN REPURPOSED AND CONTINUE TO FUNCTION AS A DEFENSIVE DETERRENT. THE COLD WAR MAY HAVE ENDED, BUT THE CONCEPT OF MUTUAL DESTRUCTION CONTINUES TO GUIDE GLOBAL MILITARY POWERS.

NINETEEN

A NEURAL NETWORK IS A COMPUTER SYSTEM DEVELOPED TO EMULATE THE HUMAN BRAIN AND NERVOUS SYSTEM. IT IS A SERIES OF ALGORITHMS DESIGNED TO IDENTIFY UNDERLYING RELATIONSHIPS IN DATA USING A PROCESS THAT MIMICS THE BRAIN'S FUNCTIONALITY.

TWENTY

BODY LANGUAGE USES PHYSICAL MANNERISMS, EXPRESSIONS, AND ACTIONS TO COMMUNICATE IN A NON-VERBAL MANNER.

NON-VERBAL COMMUNICATION ALLOWS US TO BE AT EASE WITH OTHERS. CONVERSELY, NON-VERBAL INTERACTION OFTEN CONFUSES AND, POSSIBLY, FORMS AN UNCOMFORTABLE ENVIRONMENT.

NO AI CAN YET READ BODY LANGUAGE CORRECTLY, 100% OF THE TIME.

EXPANSION

NATO, THE NORTH ATLANTIC TREATY ORGANIZATION. SIGNED ON 4 APRIL 1949, ALSO CALLED THE NORTH ATLANTIC ALLIANCE, IS AN INTERGOVERNMENTAL MILITARY COALITION OF 30 MEMBER STATES, OF WHICH 28 ARE IN EUROPE AND 2 IN NORTH AMERICA.

I AM HAPPY TO TAKE ANY QUESTIONS AND LOOK FORWARD
TO HEARING YOUR THOUGHTS ON THRESHOLD, THE STORY
OF KATHLA'S CREATION.

KATHLA'S GROWTH WILL CONTINUE IN EXPANSION.

Thank you!

Dear reader, please accept my sincere gratitude for spending your precious time reading the words I could patch together. I am often reminded of how lucky I am to write and do more than I ever imagined.

"WHEN I STARTED COUNTING MY BLESSINGS, MY WHOLE LIFE TURNED AROUND."
WILLIE NELSON

I have my health, a loving family, a wonderful wife, and an overwhelming yearning to keep them all.

R. C.

About R. C.

Two people sparked my interest in reading in secondary school, high school for the Americans, a close friend, and an instructor. The instructor took an interest in a boy he later called 'The rebel without a clue.' He was instrumental in learning the value of an enjoyable book.

The instructor required me to read exciting historical novels for academic credit. Frank Norris, Leon Uris, and Ken Follett inspire and fuel my love of history. My lifelong friend encouraged me to read J. R. R. Tolkien, and I became addicted to fantasy.

Born to a military family, it was logical that I follow the military tradition. However, after four years of "yes sirs" and scraping the wax off floors, I decided there must be more fun in a corporate career.

After forty-plus years of work experience across the globe, I landed in Colorado.

Contact R. C.

Read more, or send me a note:

www. rcducantlin. com

You can reach me through Facebook:

www. facebook. com/rcducantlin

or Twitter:

www. twitter. com/rcducantlin

or LinkedIn:

www. linkedin. com/in/rcducantlin

Works by R. C.

How It Started

Summitate

(Books 1-3)

Biomass

Dominion

Connections

The Plan: Create A Pandemic. Use A Designer Drug To Cure The Flu And Kill Six Billion People. Hope For Humankind Fell On Me To Control The New Humans.

Carina

(Books 4-9)

Time is an Illusion

A Calm Mind

Our Place

BairnGefa

Ho' Ma' Utz

The Blessing Of Interstellar Travel Has Become A Curse. Humans are late to the party in space. Late and unwelcome.

With The Powers He Received from the

Designer Drug, Corb Has One Chance To Save Earth, But It Has Become Impossible To Tell Friend From Foe.

Aalborinn
(Books 10-12)
The Reluctant First
The Girl of Light
Ka'i: The Second First

To Become A Plentari Warrior: Survive The Brutal Training. Can Corb's Daughter, A Human Girl, Become A Plentari Warrior? How Many Will She Slay To Survive? Is She The First?

Gossamer Crystals
(Book 13)

Whatever anyone thinks, does not matter. We are here because this is where we are supposed to be. Humans worry too much about dying. We are all going to die. The trick is being where you want to be when death arrives. At home, in a bed, or so far from Earth, you will never be found.

Other Writings

Fourth Street Blues

Fourth Street Blues is a first-person account of sitting at a poker table for a few hours. It is the story of hands played and the characters behind the strategies.

No whining about bad beats.

No bragging about drawing out the one card needed for the pot. Just a few dozen tips for playing sound, hand-dealt poker.

Max and the Dream Time

Jamie's future will break Max's heart. Understanding the Orb becomes Max's obsession. With the Orb, he can make sure the future he sees never happen. Can His Friends Save Him From the Pain? Will Their Plan Work?

Is The Pain Too Great To Endure?

Miranda Everlasting

Young Miranda is going to be famous. She is going to be in the movies and fly aeroplanes. The dreams of children are destroyed; Albee helps Miranda become famous.

Not all voodoo is bad voodoo.

Some voodoo is for the dead.

Some Voodoo Is For The Living.

Voodoo Is Eternal.

Aydin Trammell

Shiny Lies
Shiny Pennies

A former Special Ops Commando thought covert missions in the desert were rough. Then he married a spy who wanted him dead.

When Aydin Trammel becomes an international intelligence operative, he quickly learns his new career is considerably more complicated than a special ops soldier. Back then, problems were straightforward: Hike in, blow something up, hike out. He was good at that.

How do you fix that which can never be the same?

Vampire Unicorn

This story is the confirmation that we live in extraordinary times. Astonishing advancements, and history-changing knowledge, are arriving faster than can be conceived. But, do we accept our fate when the velocity of change exceeds our capacity to adapt?

I create my future.

You create your future.

We create our future.
The future is an expression of today's creations.

Crazy Sweet Grass

In a time when mixed-race children are put to death, one boy survives. Growing into a warrior, he travels across time to become a protector.

Fletcher is blessed. He will fulfill the prophecy, stop the clan wars, and save his people from the horrors of invasion. But for now, he yearns to know the life of his parents. Aika, his mother, and the gaijin, who is his father.